Need
Gift cert
11:00 am

Planning/ticket 3
ticket {
$43.30

Time 2:44
Adult (2) @ 15.75

Annie's
Zoo trip

1

Books by Jane O'Brien

The White Pine Trilogy:
The Tangled Roots of Bent Pine Lodge #1
The Dunes & Don'ts Antiques Emporium #2
The Kindred Spirit Bed & Breakfast #3

The Lighthouse Trilogy
The 13th Lighthouse #1
The Painted Duck #2
Owl Creek #3

The Painted Duck

The Lighthouse Trilogy Bk 2

Printed in the United States of America and
Published by: Bay Leaf Publishing

Connect with Jane O'Brien:
www.authorjaneobrien.com
www.amazon.com/author/obrienjane

Contact: authorjaneobrien@gmail.com

I want to thank all of my loyal friends, family, and fans for offering me words of encouragement during my times of doubt. I will always write, but because of you, I continue to publish. Thank you so much for helping me to achieve my dream.

Table of Contents

Whatever our souls are made of,

his and mine are the same.

Emily Bronte

Chapter One

Charity Henley stopped her car at the entrance to the long driveway of her parents' farmhouse and acreage. Whenever she came home, she would always park here a moment, and look up at the huge arch with a hanging wooden sign which declared this to be 'El Diamante Vineyard,' – The Diamond Vineyard. Her yellow Mustang convertible, a recent college graduation gift, gleamed in the Michigan sun, making a stark contrast to the naked grapevines growing in the fields. Spring had not yet brought forth the green leaves that would later produce luscious grape clusters hanging from their branches, and then at the end of summer and early fall, fill the air with the fragrance of their sweet juices.

The young woman had a love/hate relationship with the farm and that sign. Growing up, she had felt a sense of pride at belonging to one of the most prestigious families in the area. The Diamante Vineyard wine label was a national award winner several times over, and with that came status and money. She had led a life of privilege, and she would admit, at times, in her teen years, she had been a little full of herself. She was the second and youngest child, and only daughter – or so she had thought.

Five years ago, at the age of seventeen, she had met a young woman by the name of Belle who was four years older than she. They had an instant connection, and it wasn't until she brought Belle home to meet her family that her world fell apart. It was then that she discovered that Belle was her sister, and by some fluke or miracle or whatever it was, the baby girl that had been abducted from her parents twenty-one years ago, before Charity was born, had returned to them. For a moment, Charity's heart was filled with joy. She loved seeing her parents happy, and to have a newly found sister, especially her Belle, was a true gift. But then reality had set in. Charity was no longer Daddy's only little girl, and although she had retained the position of the baby of the family, Belle was the one they had ached for, for all of those years. She began to feel that she had probably been conceived as a replacement child for the stolen one.

Her brother Trey, short for Spencer Henley the Third, was crazy about Belle. He was almost five when she was taken and had always felt like it was his fault for not protecting her, so when Charity came along, he had devoted himself one hundred percent to protecting the new baby – he did not plan to lose another one. Charity began to feel that she had not only lost favoritism with her parents, but also her big brother, her loving giant and hero. Besides all of that, there was one more problem to deal with -- Brick, also known as John Brickman, Junior, attorney at law, Trey's best friend, and the love of Charity's life since she could first talk. Brick was nine years her senior, and she had been determined to make him her own when she was old enough. As soon as she could express her feelings, at the ripe old age of three, she told Brick she was going to marry him someday. They all thought it was a silly little girl's crush, but to her it was a reality. She prayed every night that he would wait for her to grow up, so their age difference would not seem so great. But he met Belle before she had a chance; he was actually the one who was instrumental in finding her big sister and bringing her back home. Once Brick laid his eyes on the beautiful Belle, he could see no others. Charity held out hope, but when they were married last year, she finally had to give up on her dream. The pain was excruciating still, and made homecomings especially difficult.

Charity took one more look at the sign. She had lived here all of her life, helped prune the grapevines and worked in the winery side by side with her dad, learning the business for the time she would inherit along with her brother. She was reminded that this was her home, too. It wasn't until that fateful night that Belle had come to dinner, that Charity had become aware of the fact that the vineyard was named for her sister, because of the diamond-shaped birthmark on her inner arm. For years, after Belle was taken, it was called El Diamante Perdido – The Lost Diamond -- but her parents had removed the word 'Perdido' in celebration of her homecoming. And there lay the push/pull of her feelings. On one hand she loved Belle, her best friend and sibling, and she knew she would always love Brick, the man of her fantasies since childhood; while on the other hand, she hated them both for destroying her dreams.

The engine roared and the tires spun the gravel as Charity angrily jammed her foot on the accelerator, but she soon let up, knowing her father would not approve of her driving style, and if she tore up the driveway there would be hell to pay. She had called ahead to tell them of her arrival, and she had expected her mother to be anxiously waiting on the porch swing as she usually was whenever she came home. But instead the porch was empty and a pickup truck was parked directly in front of the steps. More than a little annoyed, she got out of the now dusty Mustang and began the task of unloading her bags and dragging them into the house. 'Where was everyone?' she thought. 'Couldn't someone have been interested enough in her return to help?'

Charity slammed the door hard, making sure someone would hear her arrival. She waited a moment to see if anyone would come running out, but there was not one stir from within. With a flip of her hand she forced the hair out of her eyes, and at the same time she exhaled loudly past her puckered lips. She slowly dragged her feet as she walked to the back of the car, hoping against hope that someone would come out to help her. Charity almost left her things in the car for later, when her strong ox of a brother would lift each bag as if they were filled with feathers, but then she decided she would go ahead and try it herself. When she had moved out of her dorm, there was no end to eligible young men who were eager to help her; she didn't even have to ask. She just struggled a little and one of them would jump right in, offering his services. Of course, they always asked for her number after the job was accomplished, but she had long ago invented a fake phone number that she could rattle off if the guy wasn't interesting enough for her, which he usually wasn't. That way she didn't have to deal with his hurt feelings when she turned him away. But there were no young men on the prowl here, so she tugged and pulled the heavy bag on wheels up the steps while walking backwards, banging it loudly on each riser, until she was finally on the large, wrap-around, front porch.

'Strange,' she thought, 'the house is eerily quiet.' She paused a moment to catch her breath and gaze out at the grapevines growing below. This was her favorite view and the one her mother had selected for the front door placement when they had first built the farmhouse, almost thirty years ago. Her father had often brought up the subject of building a new house on this very spot. He said he'd like it to be modern with lots of glass, high ceilings, and fieldstone. He had planned to show off their success; he wanted plenty of room to entertain all of their out-of-town clients. But Hope, Charity's mother, had always refused. This was the house where she had raised her children and this was the house she wanted them to come home to. Any of their guests could either stay in the condo in Frankfort at the beach on Lake Michigan, or in one of the spare rooms here, she had said. After a few years of nudging and prodding, it was obvious that her mother was not going to budge on the subject, so her father, Spencer Henley, had given up. He knew when to back down to keep his woman happy.

After one more tug, Charity decided to leave the heavy suitcase on the porch for either her father or brother to move later. She slowly pulled open the screen door to the dark house, but before she had a chance to let her eyes adjust from the bright sun, she was shocked by loud cheers of "Surprise!" Her eyes instantly filled with tears. They had not forgotten her at all. She should have guessed, but a bout of petulance had taken over her usual agreeable disposition. Charity involuntarily took a step back; she was truly overwhelmed as they all rushed forward to greet her.

They were laughing at her stunned look and tried to soften the blow with hugs and kisses. She had to admit that she had been totally surprised. Her mother, Esperanza Salazar Henley – known only as Hope -- reached her first. She was a petite, dark-haired woman who never seemed to lose her beauty. "Welcome home, my darling. We've missed you."

"Thank you, mama. I missed you, too. And you know I missed your home cooking."

The next one to reach her was her father, Spencer Henley, Junior. He wrapped her in a big bear hug. He smelled just like the daddy she knew as a little girl. Charity was glad that some things never changed. "How's my little girl? We're so glad you're home. I hope you're planning on staying with us. Mama's got your room all ready for you."

"Oh, daddy, of course I'll stay. But I can't stay forever. You knew after graduation I would have to move on with my life."

"Of course, but let's not talk about that now. I need to keep my daughter with me for a little while yet."

Trey pushed his father aside. Her big brother, the one who was always there for her, picked her up and twirled her around. "My goodness, Trey, I wasn't that far away," Charity said, laughing through her tears.

"Yeah, but I couldn't pick on you, and now I can, whenever I feel like it. Seriously, it's good to have you home."

A few months ago, Trey had returned from a four-year stint in the military. According to her parents it had been rocky for a little while. The adjustment, they said, had not been easy for him. "Thanks, Trey. It feels good to me, too. But how are you these days? Everything going okay?"

Trey tensed for a second. He didn't like being reminded. "Absolutely, I'm fine. I'm enjoying a quiet life now – just me and the grapes," he laughed. Charity looked intently at his face as he talked. He did seem like his old self. 'Good. Maybe they were over that hump,' she thought.

Next to come forward was her sister, Belle. "Charity, I'm so happy you're finished with school and back home. I missed our long talks and walks."

"There were plenty of late night talks on the phone, as I recall."

"Yes, but it's never the same unless you can look a person in the eye. And Skype and Facetime just don't measure up. Let's try to get off by ourselves later. I want to hear all about your plans." Belle smiled at her sweetly and squeezed her hand.

Charity's beautiful sister had so many similarities to herself, but she never felt as though she could compete with her striking good looks. Ever since Belle had come into their lives again, Charity had felt as though she were 'the other Henley girl,' although nothing could be further from the truth. Charity had been a Henley for 17 years when Belle returned home after being stolen as a baby. Belle had technically only been in this family for four years, now. But whenever Charity looked at Belle, she saw the gorgeous dark-haired woman she had first met in Grand Haven, the woman she aspired to grow up to be like. But at that time she didn't know they were sisters, and that they were destined to be family forever.

Over Belle's shoulder, Charity could see the next person in line waiting to greet and congratulate her. She sucked in a deep breath. This one was always difficult. Brick, Belle's husband, stepped forward, completely unaware of Charity's feelings for him. He pulled her in for a hug, and she melted into his arms. He felt so good. He smelled so good. Would she ever get over the excited flutter followed by a sinking feeling when she realized he could never be hers? Tears filled her eyes as they usually did whenever she thought of him.

"Hello, Brick. How are you?" Charity said softly.

"I'm great. It's good to have you home. I'll bet you're glad to finally be done with those classes."

"Yes, that's going to be a big change in my life. No more studying." She laughed, taking a moment to compose herself.

"You look beautiful, Charity. These local guys are going to go crazy when they catch a glimpse of you."

"Thanks, Brick, but I'm not in the market just yet. I might never be. I have other things on my mind right now."

"Oh? I'd like to hear about that."

"Later, okay?"

"Of course, you've got others to greet. I think every relative and friend you have is here already or on the way." He glanced over his shoulder. "Hey, Trey, let's get those suitcases off the porch before someone trips on them."

"Sure. I can give you a hand with that. We can move the truck now, too. There's no reason to leave it there any longer. I think we accomplished our goal of frustrating Charity." Trey gave Charity a grin and a wink.

Charity wistfully watched Brick's back as he walked away with Trey. She would never give up hope, but if anything came of her love for Brick, it would mean her sister would have a broken heart, and then how would she be able to deal with that?

Just as a frown began to form on her forehead, Hope stepped forward inviting everyone to dig in to the food on the buffet table. "We're set up in the back yard with tents, tables, and chairs, so you can carry your plates out there if you like, or feel free to stay in the house."

Charity stood back and watched as everyone began to talk to each other, as they filed towards her mother's home cooking. She smelled enchiladas, fiery homemade salsa, and burritos. Next to the Mexican food she discovered her German grandma's potato salad recipe along with her famous baked beans. There was also a bakery cake with writing congratulating her on her accomplishment. Her mother had gone all out. It was good to be home. She realized how well-planned this party was. They had done a great job of keeping it all a secret. She knew how lucky she was to have such an amazing family, and she felt grateful.

Charity turned to look out the door as the boys gathered up her suitcases; she held the screen door open for them as they struggled to get the heavy cases in the house.

"Holy cow, Charity," said Trey, "what have you got in these things? A ship anchor? But the bigger question is, how did you get them on the porch in the first place?"

Charity raised up her arms in a fighter's stance and said, "I ain't no wimp. Get used to it." They all laughed good-heartedly. It was something she had said when she was a child when she was being picked on one time by her brother. She had said it in front of some out-of-town company. Seeing the tiny, little, dark-haired girl look so tough had brought the house down. She had not been allowed to forget that phrase since. At first she felt silly and humiliated whenever her family brought it up, but now she took it as her own personal motto.

Charity was proud of her toughness. She would never let anyone push her around. But underneath all the bravado was a heart of gold, and a tenderness she very rarely let anyone see anymore. She had shown it to Belle, trusted her with her feelings, only to find out that they were both in love with the same man. The day Belle and Brick got married was probably the worst day of her life. As tough as she liked to think she was, she didn't think she would ever get over that.

"Charity!" She turned, when she heard her name called out by a female voice, to see her best friend in the whole world -- Sid. Sid's blonde hair and blue eyes were a stark contrast to her own dark features. Where Charity was somber and introspective at times, Sid was always cheerful and upbeat. The moment they first met in first grade they became instant friends. Charity had offered Sid a piece of candy out of her own sticky hand, and they discovered they shared a love of root beer barrels. Sid, whose real name was Sharon Ilene

Davidson, was christened by Charity as Sid in the 6th grade when Sharon was lamenting that she hated her first name. She said she didn't look like a Sharon and she didn't feel like a Sharon. She wondered what in the world her parents had been thinking. Charity immediately suggested combining her initials to form Sid. Sharon loved it, and after informing her parents of her newly chosen name, she was Sid from that day on, and it was all she had been known as ever since.

The two friends hugged and laughed, even though it had only been a few weeks since Sid had come to visit Charity in Grand Rapids. It was only a two-and-half-hour drive to the Grand Valley State University GR Campus, but it had been quite a feat the first time Sid had done it by herself. Grand Rapids was quite a bit different than the sleepy town of Frankfort. It had meant conquering the traffic at speeds she was not used to driving, right through the heart of the city. But she had managed quite well, so she tried to visit every month or so. And the girls saw each other when Charity came home.

Originally, when Charity had first applied to GVSU she had thought she would be attending the campus in Allendale. The college had been built in a quiet farming community in 1960 and was about 12 miles west of the second biggest city in the state. Charity assumed she would be close to Lake Michigan and therefore feel more at home, but she soon found out that the business administration major with a minor in marketing that she was seeking could only be had at the extension campus in Grand Rapids. It now included so many buildings it was almost as large as the original campus. It had seemed a little scary in the beginning, but she soon adapted to the busier lifestyle. A large warehouse had been turned into a beautiful residence hall, which of course her father could afford to house her in. And she loved being close to the quaint downtown coffee shops, restaurants, and bars. When Sid came to visit they enjoyed walking the city and exploring new places on Monroe Street. The bars were only a place to hang out for both of them, somewhere to meet friends. Sid rarely drank, and Charity had grown up with alcohol always present in the home, so she never felt the need to get drunk like some of her classmates had. She looked at wine as a beverage to be had with dinner or as her parents did when they sipped it in front of the fireplace in the evening. She never understood the purpose of getting so drunk she was no longer in control. For that, her father had been grateful. At least that was one thing he didn't have to worry about while she was gone.

"Sid," said Charity, "let's grab some food and go outside. I can't promise an uninterrupted chat yet, but we can try."

"I was thinking the same thing. But I'm just so happy you are home and we can see each other more often."

The girls loaded up their plates with the wonderful combination of Mexican- American and

German-American foods that were favorites of the family. They weren't the least concerned about carbs or sugars. They were young and active. It was a time in their life when a few extra pounds could be easily burned off with a run or a trip to the gym. They carried their plates out the back door and settled on two folding chairs under a large oak tree. The ever present breeze coming off of Lake Michigan provided this late spring day just the right amount of air movement to keep insects at bay.

"So," said Charity with a mouthful of food, "how is the new job at the doctor's office? Are you enjoying nursing as much as you thought you would?"

"Yes, I really love it. You know it's all I ever wanted to do. And the doctor's office is just right for me. The pace is steady, but nothing like what I would face in a hospital. And the best part is that I can stay in Frankfort. I was so lucky to get this job. There were quite a few others who applied."

"Well, of course you would get it. They recognized a good nurse when they saw one."

"Thank you, Charity. That means a lot to me. But now, what's next for you? Do you have plans for the future? I know you had thought about leaving the area and getting away from your family. Where will you go?"

"You know, Sid, I think I've changed my mind. At first, all I could think of was getting farther away from Belle and Brick. I wasn't looking to move away from my parents and Trey, really. I still have feelings for Brick and I always will, but I think I can handle it. After all, they live in Traverse City, but I'd have to see them at family functions anyway, no matter where I moved. So I think I'll stay around and see how it goes."

Sid let out a little squeal. She squeezed Charity's hand, and said, "I'm so happy. I've missed seeing you every day. Skyping and Facetiming just isn't the same." A slight frown appeared on her pretty round face. "What are your plans, then? There's not much to offer here."

"I haven't approached Daddy yet, but I have a proposition for him. I think he'll go for it, because he was always hoping I would join the business, but he knew better than to force me into it. I want to use my new skills to help market the Diamante Vineyard brand."

"I think he's going to love the idea. Actually, it's probably what he wanted all along. When will you approach him about it?"

Charity bit her lip a little; the timing had to be just right or he would think it was his idea and she would always feel under his thumb. "I'm not sure but I'll have to move fast. Probably tomorrow morning, after all of this homecoming hoopla has calmed down."

"Good plan. Let me know as soon as you talk to him. I'm off tomorrow, so maybe we can get together again later."

"Sounds like a plan."

"Charity," called her mother. "I need you to meet someone."

"Sorry, Sid, I have to do my duties and do a meet-and-greet. I'll call first thing in the morning after I talk to Dad."

Chapter Two

Family and friends stayed until dusk, and then one or two at a time, they drifted back to their own busy lives, leaving behind dirty dishes, half-empty glasses, and unfinished cake. Overall, Charity had enjoyed herself immensely. She never minded being the star of the show. Attention was not something she had ever craved, but she didn't shy from it, either. She had always been an open and friendly person, so people naturally gravitated to her. They had all wanted to be there to wish her well. She had fielded the questions about her future quite easily with jokes and banter, because she wanted to talk to her father first before she let her idea out of the bag.

Hope was in the kitchen cleaning up a few things, and even though they had all offered to help, she persuaded them to sit in the family room and relax. Most of them had been at her beck and call all day whenever something was needed. They knew she must be just as exhausted as they were, but they also knew better than to argue. Hope would remain in the kitchen. Nothing could persuade her to stop moving until the last of the cleanup was completed.

When she was finally ready to join them, she offered everyone a glass of wine, and a few leftover snacks. Trey and Belle took soft drinks. She noticed that Belle was looking quite tired and a little pasty, especially when she had brought in the tray of food. "Are you okay, Belle? Would you like to lie down?"

"I'm fine, Mama. I guess I overdid it. I chased around a few preschoolers this morning before we came and wore myself out before I got here."

"How do you like social work, now that you've had a chance to fully immerse yourself in it?" asked Charity.

Belle smiled. "I really love it, but sometimes it just breaks my heart to see how some people live. And of course, it often reminds me of my own upbringing when my mother – Karen, I mean, sorry Mama --" she glanced at Hope –"had difficulties in providing for me. I will forever be grateful that she was a good mother, even though we were so poor. Some of these children don't get the proper nurturing they need. I don't think I can ever thank you enough, Mama and Daddy, for putting me through college so I could get my degree in social work." She smiled tiredly at them both.

Charity still cringed sometimes to hear Belle call her father 'daddy.' It seemed to her that name should be reserved for use by someone who had been raised and loved by a special father. But Belle had not known how to address her parents, after she had been stolen by Karen as a baby, and so she had followed Charity's lead. When she returned to the family after being gone for twenty-one years, she felt awkward addressing them by their proper names. When she had tried out the names Charity used, she saw the pleased expressions on their faces, and so she had continued, because she wanted to give them the happiness they had lost for so long. They were truly wonderful people and deserved anything she could do to give back.

Suddenly Belle turned green; she quickly jumped up and ran to the bathroom. "Is she okay?" asked Hope with concern in her voice.

"She'll be fine," said Brick. "Just give her a minute. She's had a rough day." He glanced in the direction she had gone wondering if he should go after her.

Charity loved sitting across from him like this, because it gave her the opportunity to gaze on his handsome face. Usually, she only looked at him furtively, so the rest of the family would not guess the depth of her love for him, but sitting across the room on the sofa like this, she could allow herself to dream of what might have been. Charity didn't realize it, but Trey caught her look, a slight frown creasing his forehead; he vowed to have a little talk with her, later.

Belle returned in just a few minutes; she looked at Brick and gave a slight nod, giving him reassurance that she was all right. Just then, it dawned on Charity that Belle had turned down wine all day, claiming that she was so tired it would just put her to sleep. She suddenly had a sickening feeling in the pit of her stomach.

Brick reached for Belle's hand as she sat next to him on the couch. He cleared his throat. "We have an announcement to make, but we were hoping to save it because we didn't want to rain on Charity's parade. But I realize, now that you've witnessed some of Belle's strange behavior, you would probably guess, anyway. So we're--"

Belle interrupted him, unable to stay out of it any longer. "We're going to have a baby," she said a little shyly. At first there was silence, and then a big cheer erupted --all except for Charity who was in shock. How dare they? How could they? Now all hope was lost, for sure. She could never have Brick. Once in a while she would allow a tiny thought to creep into her mind about trying to take Brick away from Belle, but she knew it would destroy her family, and so she had kept her feelings to herself. 'What's wrong with me?' she asked herself. 'Stop it, stop it,' she screamed inside her head. She put her hand to her forehead involuntarily, composed herself, took a deep breath and smiled while giving her congratulations. Everyone else was so full of joy, no one seemed to notice, or so she thought. Trey knew his sister well, though, and recognized the pain on her face.

Hope was crying and laughing at the same time. "Oh, my darling, I'm going to be a grandmother. How wonderful. When are you due?"

"Our due date is December 15th, so we're planning on a Christmas baby," said Brick with a grin.

"You did it, man," said Trey as he hugged Brick. "You're going to be a dad. Maybe Uncle Trey can teach the kid to throw a decent ball, better than you, anyway."

As the men began to talk about the pros and cons of having a boy versus a girl, Belle and her mother discussed morning sickness, and body changes that were bound to happen. Charity did her best to comment and listen, but the whole time she felt as if she had lost the biggest race of her life and she was banned from ever competing again. It was then that she knew her future, as she had always planned, was truly over. She would never marry – she wouldn't allow herself to. She would never have children of her own – she didn't want them if they weren't hers and Brick's. She would have to figure out how to live the rest of her years on this Earth without a lifetime companion – without him. She would go through the motions, date, maybe even take on lovers, but she would never allow herself to have a long-term commitment again. One-sided loves rarely worked, and obviously, after loving Brick for years, she could see that there was no guarantee that a man would return the love he was given.

As Charity's head was reeling with the loss of Brick, she also felt another strong and powerful emotion. She knew this was the one she should focus on – she was going to be an aunt! As soon as that realization set in, she felt the joy she should have experienced at the beginning of the announcement.

She vowed to keep this thought in the forefront and push all negative thoughts behind her. Aunt Charity. It sounded nice, real nice. She rose to hug her sister, vowing to be the best aunt in the whole wide world.

Chapter Three

The house was quiet, since Belle and Brick had left for their home in Traverse City, and Trey had headed into town to The Painted Duck to meet friends. The only sounds to be heard now were coming from the kitchen -- clattering dishes, running water, and a happy grandmother-to-be humming as she worked. Hope was in her element, putting leftover food in storage containers, stacking dishes in the dishwasher, and cleaning countertops. She would never allow herself to go to bed until the kitchen was spotless. Charity was constantly amazed with her mother's energy.

Charity had offered her help more than once this evening, but her mother said this party had been for her, and she didn't need to take part in cleaning up this time. Hope encouraged her daughter to spend some quiet time with her father. When Charity sat next to her dad on the sofa, he pulled her in, putting his arm around her. "How's my girl?"

"I'm great, Dad. It feels good to be home."

"We missed you," said Spencer, adding a kiss on the forehead. "Are you planning to stay a while? You've never said what your future plans are."

"I'd really like to talk to you about that. I was hoping to wait until morning, but if you're up for it we could start the discussion now." Charity looked at her father hopefully, then slid across from him to the opposite chair. This talk should be more business-like, and she knew she would not get the respect she wanted curled up next to her father like a child. She sat up straight hoping to convey to him that she was actually a grown woman, now, with skills and training.

Spencer looked deeply at his daughter. She had come a long way since those rebellious teen years. He was proud of the woman he was seeing across from him now. "This sounds serious. Should I be worried?"

"Not at all. It's a good thing. Well, I think so, and I think you will, too, if you give me a chance." She took a deep breath and continued on with her idea. "I want to stay and work with you and Trey at the vineyard and winery." *Great Response !!*

"What? That's wonderful but not what I expected at all." The big man sat up straight, a wide smile spreading across his face. Nothing would make him happier than to keep his children close, especially this girl who held a tender spot in his heart. "How could you be worried about telling me that?"

"Well, because it's different than you might think. I don't want to be another field hand or errand runner. I've had four long years of college, and I think I'm prepared for a new role. No, I know I am." Charity was almost afraid to go on. How she presented her plan was crucial to how he would accept it. She knew he still thought of her as his little girl. Trey was the one who had been groomed to take over someday. She was meant to get married and maybe help with the bills like her mother had done. But she knew she had more in her than that, lots more.

"Dad, I have an idea, and I've been thinking about it for a long time, way before I went to college, actually. I'd like to become your marketing agent, your brand promoter. I don't think you do enough to reach the public. It's always been pretty much word of mouth with a few ads here and there. I think we can do a lot better. I'm bursting with thoughts and plans, and I'd like to go over them with you tomorrow."

Great response!

"My, that's not what I expected at all. I thought, after your education was completed, you might want to leave us for a big city. It makes me happy and proud to know you're willing to stay here with us."

"Whoa, not stay with you exactly. That's not what I meant. I plan to get my own place. I want to work for you, or work with you. I want a title and a good salary, so I can afford that place. I intend to be on my own, but I want to be involved in the family business. I was thinking of 'Head of Marketing and Research'. How does that sound?"

Spencer was surprised. Apparently, she had given this a lot of thought. He turned over what she had said in his mind for a moment, then said, "Okay, if you want to be taken seriously, then in the morning we can sit down in the office, and you can present your proposal. I'd like to hear your ideas and plans for our future, as well as anything else you would expect out of the job. Let's keep this strictly business, and then I'll make my decision."

"Thanks, Dad, that's all I want. I intend to make sure I will be treated the same as you would any of your other employees. If you don't like what I have to say, we can move on, and I'll look for work elsewhere."

They stood up and shook hands, then laughed and hugged. Behind Charity's back, Spencer was beaming. Behind Spencer's back, Charity was beaming.

Charity's dream was the same one it had been for the last ten years. It was always about a handsome young man with laughing eyes. He would tease her like a brother, but then he would finally see her as a grown woman and instantly fall in love with her. He would twirl her around and declare his undying love. It was a childish dream, and therefore bound for disaster. This morning, when she woke up to dried tears on her face and pillow, she truly knew that it was over. She would never have that same dream again. Brick was forever lost to her. When she sat up in bed, the lingering shadows of the story in her head gave her a slight headache. She resolved that she would never let a man touch her heart in the way that Brick had. Overnight, her outgoing, friendly attitude was gone; she had built a protective wall around herself, the strength of The Great Wall of China. She resolved to be a good sister and sister-in-law and a wonderful aunt, but that was it. There would be no men in her life – ever. The hurt was too much to take, because even though she sometimes had come off as a tough kid, she was the most sensitive one in the family. She was sure this latest wound would never heal.

The smell of bacon, and most probably blueberry pancakes, wafted up the stairs. Mama would be at the stove already, eager to please her daughter with her favorite breakfast. And then after breakfast she would sit down with her father and discuss her new ideas. Charity instantly perked up at the thought of starting her new life in the family business, and if all went well, she would have a position and a title and she would be off to a good start right out of college. Who could ask for more? It was something to be grateful for, so she decided she would focus on that, in order to clear the cobwebs from her mind.

She took a hot shower, then combed out her long, dark, wet tresses, considering once again as she did every few months, as to whether or not she should cut it shorter. Did the long hair make her look childish, she wondered? All through school, boys had been fascinated with her hair. It was an asset she had learned to use when necessary. And now that she wasn't going to need ways to attract the opposite sex, perhaps shorter was the better choice. But after blowing it dry and twisting it into a thick creation at the back of her head, she thought it looked rather professional. She decided she would keep it that way for a while and see how she liked it.

Now to choose her outfit. This morning was no time for shorts or jeans. She selected her black dress slacks and a short-sleeve, beige sweater, then added a long gold chain and gold hoop earrings. She was pleased with the look, and she was sure her father would be impressed.

Her mother heard her tread on the stairs as she came down. She turned and almost dropped her whisk. "Uh, good morning," she stuttered. "My, don't you look nice."

Her father looked up from the newspaper he was reading. "Whoa! Where's my little girl with messy hair and pajamas? Good morning, Charity."

"Good morning," she said cheerily. She was pleased with their reaction. "I've been up for a while and decided you should have the pleasure of a fully-clothed child at the table for a change." She bent down to kiss her father on the forehead. "Besides, I have a meeting with Daddy this morning. Right?"

"We do? Oh, I thought you were just rambling last night." he said.

Charity's face fell. Would they never take her seriously?

"Just kidding, honey. I'm looking forward to hearing what you have to say."

"Oh, Dad. Why do I always fall for that routine?"

He laughed out loud, loving that he had pulled it off once again. Charity had always been so easy to tease. Hope brought the steaming hot plate of pancakes to the table. She set down a fresh container of warm maple syrup next to it along with the crispy bacon, which was right on the edge of being burned, just the way Charity liked it. "Mama, you remembered."

Hope patted her on the shoulder and smiled. "Of course, I remembered. I was always grateful that someone would eat my overcooked bacon, and I could pretend I did it on purpose." She sighed as she sat at the table. She looked her daughter straight in the eye, and said, "Seriously, it's so good to have you home. I missed seeing your face every day."

"Me too, Mama. I missed you both a lot, but now I'm here. So let's eat."

The breakfast conversation was smooth and easy, even though Charity was as nervous as a June bug in a henhouse, as her grandma used to say. She had managed to keep her cool, but now she was sitting across from her large, imposing father at the desk in his home office. It was the same office they were never allowed to enter as children, so just being in this room was intimidating. Even though she loved him dearly, she respected him so much it scared her sometimes. She had always wanted so badly to please him, and during those years when they thought they had lost Belle forever, Charity had always felt like a replacement child -- a child who had no chance of ever competing with the image of the beautiful baby they had had hopes and dreams for. Today, she planned on changing their view of her forever, even though that view was coming from her perception only, because her parents actually adored her. She would prove she had something Belle did not – business savvy. She was sure her father would see her in a new light once she laid it all out for him.

"Well, now, tell what me this is all about. I'm curious to hear your proposal." Spencer had every intention of hiring his daughter in some capacity, but he rather enjoyed watching her squirm. It wasn't like her. She was usually so self-assured; he decided her idea must mean a great deal to her. Maybe she had grown up, at last. He leaned back into his reclining leather desk chair and put both hands on the back of his head, elbows out. Charity recognized the pose. It was the one he went to whenever he was concentrating or in deep thought. She finally felt ready to proceed.

"I have everything laid out for you on this spreadsheet." She pushed it toward him, but he didn't make a move to accept it yet.

"A spreadsheet? You had time to do all of that?" He was surprised at her effort.

"Like I said, I've been thinking about this for quite a while. I worked on it at college in my spare time, so I could have it ready for you." He detected a slight tremor in her voice. She was more nervous than he had first thought.

"Go ahead. Tell me about it before I look at the papers. I want to hear your version first."

"Well, you know I've grown up following you around, and I know quite a bit about the business, but once I went to college, I realized that all I knew was from a child's point of view. The talk I heard around the dinner table was about grapes, weather, harvest, bottling equipment, etc. I never once thought about sales and how the wine went from our farm to a retail outlet. I never questioned how people decided to buy our product. It was there, a fact of life. I would go in a store and see our bottles on the shelf. But now my eyes have been opened. I understand a lot about marketing to the public. I've been trained in all aspects from presentation to advertising."

"Interesting so far; go on," said her father.

"I love our logo and I love our labeling. The design is outstanding. There's not a thing to change there."

"Well, I'm glad for that," he said with a tolerant smile.

Charity chose to ignore his sarcasm and went on. "Over the last few times I've come home on break, Sid and I have visited other wineries. We've taken tours, sampled wines, and even made some purchases. I watched how the process was handled by our competitors and then compared it to our own business. Here are some notes I made." She shoved another paper across the desk. Charity waited a moment while her father glanced over the sheet.

"You discovered all of this? If it's true, it's amazing and a little disconcerting at the same time. It looks like we are falling short on customer service."

"Yes, and that's only the beginning. Our showroom needs a lot of updating. Right now we're still using barn wood and rustic tiles, as our design, but I think we need to bring the colors and style up to the twenty-first century. I suggest a whole new makeover – I have sketches for that also, but I must say, Dad, we're falling behind the others in the race to keep up."

"Hmm, you may have a point. Nothing's been done to the showroom in years."

"That's just the tip of the iceberg. I'd like to see satellite showrooms in other cities. All of the other wineries are doing it. There are tasting rooms in Grand Rapids for Traverse City wines."

"Really? I wasn't aware of that," added Spencer. He was beginning to realize that Charity might be on to something.

Charity was feeling a little more confident now, so she decided to push forward. "That's just the beginning of my ideas. Once we accomplish this, I think we should look at keeping the homey tradition going here on the property. We need to have adult hayrides in the fall ending back at our tasting room, clean up the old barn, and hold elegant rustic weddings where only our own wines will be served. We can host meet-and-greets for young singles, sort of a place to meet the one you'll spend the rest of your life with. Maybe even host an annual food tasting event, served with our very own wines, of course. We can decorate the barn so even Martha Stewart would approve. Dad, with the proper advertising, the possibilities are endless. And I know how to do that, too. I graduated top of my class, you know." Charity decided she had better slow down. Maybe this was all he could take for one meeting. It was a lot to lay on him at once.

"You know, Mother and I have actually talked about a hayride, but there was never enough time to organize it and host the thing. I actually like your ideas, although I know we can't do them all at once. If you agree to take one thing at a time and go slow, I'll offer you head of Marketing and Research, just as you requested. We can work out the salary later. I need to come up with a budget for you, and I'll expect you to keep it in line. For the first year, I'll want a monthly report promptly on my desk on the first, and after that, if all goes well, I'll expect a quarterly report." Spencer could see that Charity was trying to control her excitement, but he didn't want to go too easy on her, so he added, "You know, this is not a game. It's our bread and butter. We've built a good reputation in the wine industry over the years, and I don't want to see that spoiled. I'll have to discuss everything you've laid out, here, with your mother and Trey. They're decision-makers, too. I'll inform Belle about it. Even though she doesn't have much interest or knowledge in the vineyard, she should be in on any big changes like this. How does that sound? Do we have an agreement?"

"That's perfect, Dad. It's all I ever wanted. I'm thrilled that you're willing to take a chance on me." She stood and shook hands, the same way they had last night, and then she ran around the desk and buried her face in his big strong chest. She vowed she would prove to them that she could do it, and nothing would stop her from being the best marketing agent they had ever had.

Chapter Four

The man watched her across the room. He liked watching her gestures as she told her story to her friend. They laughed occasionally, and he was mesmerized with her smile. He was slumped down in the corner booth at The Painted Duck, so he was sure she couldn't see him watching. It was his favorite spot whenever he came here, because it allowed him a great view of the door; he could see the comings and goings of the customers, and that was just the way he liked it. He always positioned himself in this way whenever he was in public so he could see everything around him. It had become habit.

He nursed his beer and nibbled on his burger, one of the best around, but he no longer cared about the food in front of him, once he saw her. He had come in here to solve a problem, and for that he needed to be alone. That was easy. He was a loner, so not too many people even noticed he was there, which was exactly what he preferred.

Her hair was long and dark, just the way he remembered. Just the way he had liked it. Her skin was perfection, and those big dark eyes could make any man go weak in the knees. Every once in a while, when the music died down and other conversations around him were at a lull, he could hear her voice. It stirred memories he had tried to forget.

He pulled his black ball cap lower on his head, the brim covering most of his face. He extended his long legs out under the table and slumped lower. He wore jeans and a black tee shirt which stretched tightly over his muscle-hardened chest. His red plaid shirt hung open, just like so many other young men in the bar. He was hoping she wouldn't notice him; he preferred to observe at this point. Maybe later he would find a way to insert himself into her life. He planned to take it slow. It was the only way to handle things. He knew she wouldn't accept him any other way. He knew her that well.

The Painted Duck was a favorite of the locals and in the summer it swelled to capacity with tourists. It had one entrance in the front which opened into a wind-blocking vestibule. The interior door on the right went to The Painted Duck Steakhouse, one of the finest dining establishments around; prices on the menu were high, suggesting if you had to look at the price column, you probably shouldn't be there. But the door to the left went into The Painted Duck Bar & Grill. This was where the locals hung out. The food served there was plain bar food -- burgers, hotdogs, nachos, and wings – just enough required by the State to help prevent intoxication. The lighting was darker on this side -- the mood a little more jovial, the music a tad bit louder. The TV was permanently set to a sports channel, causing the patrons to erupt in cheers every once in a while, but overall, it was just a quiet neighborhood bar. A gathering place for friends.

Charity and Sid sat at a table in the middle of the room. They were totally unaware that they were being observed. Neither one of them ever drank much, so they were sipping on Cokes, having already polished off their burgers and fries. Charity was twirling her straw around and round in her tall glass, while Sid listened intently. Charity had just gone over the plan she had presented to her father, point by point. Sid was a good and supportive friend, so she listened carefully, making comments along the way.

"I'm so happy he's giving you a chance;" said Sid. "For one thing you deserve it, and for another, that means we'll be living near each other again."

The girls reached out to squeeze each other's hands. "So," asked Charity, "how are the wedding plans coming along? Is there anything I can do to help at this point?"

Sid giggled. "We're a long way from that. We haven't even set a date yet."

"Why not? What's the delay?" asked Charity. "You guys have known each other forever."

"Yeah, but you know Hank. He likes to take his time. And we have so many things to line up first. We want to be settled in our jobs, and then we need to build a bank account. I don't want to depend on my parents to pay for a wedding. You know them; they'd go all out, and they can't afford it."

"I understand wanting to do it on your own, but don't forget to let family and friends take some of the burden. That's what we're here for." Charity and Sid had been through some pretty tough times together -- boys, family arguments, and boys again. They always had each other's backs.

Sid looked at her with a sweet smile. "I promise, when the time is right, I'll involve you completely."

"Wonderful, that's all I ask." Charity glanced at her watch. "I'd better get going. It's getting late. Mama worries. I can't wait to get my own place, so no one will be watching my comings and goings every minute. I love those people to death, but I feel like I just got out of prison and I'm in a half-way house." She stood up and pushed back her chair.

Sid laughed. "I know what you mean. I guess they just don't want us to grow up yet. Maybe we'll understand when we're mothers ourselves."

"That probably won't happen for me, Sid. You know I'm never getting married."

"What are you talking about? Sit back down. I guess we're not done yet. You've never mentioned this to me before."

"I was trying not to bring it up. I've decided to be a single career woman for the rest of my life."

"What? Why?"

"Belle's pregnant," she said quietly.

Sid clapped her hands together. "Oh, that's wonderful. You're going to be an aunt! But wait. What does that have to do with anything? You're not still hung up on Brick, are you?"

"I've always loved him, you know that. And when I found out about the baby last night, it really hit home. He belongs to her and always will. They'll be completely cemented once the baby arrives. I'll never have a chance."

"And that's how it should be. Charity, face it, you never really had a chance. We've talked about this before. Brick is nine years older than you are, and he's always thought of you as a kid. And then once he met Belle, there was no one else for him."

The man watched as she sat back down and noticed the mood change. Something serious had just happened. He studied their body language trying to figure it out. He caught a word here and there as their voices carried across the room during a dead spot in the music, but it wasn't enough to make out what they were talking about. He liked this intense side of her. It suited him better. He shifted slightly to get a better view. Something stirred in him that he hadn't felt in a long time -- an urgency, a need, a burning desire. Time was running out for him. He decided he would make his move sooner than later. She stood up once again, and so did he. It was time for the approach.

"You're right, Sid. I know that in my heart, but it's difficult. I'll get through it. Thanks for grounding me like you always do." Charity rose from the table, picked up her purse and cell phone. She leaned down to hug her friend. "Now, I really do have to go." She spun quickly on her heals trying to hide her tears from Sid, causing her to bump hard into a tall, very good-looking, man. She literally fell into his arms; her face was in his chest. "Oh, excuse me, I'm so sorry. I'm such a klutz."

He laughed. "Not a problem. I'll let you fall into my arms any day," he said with a smooth, buttery voice.

Charity looked up into the green eyes and blond hair of a very familiar face. It was a few years older, but otherwise he hadn't changed much at all.

"Tucker Morrison?" Charity straightened herself to an upright position.

"Charity? Wow, how are you?" He was tall and well-built. She noticed that much was the same. He glanced at the table. "Oh, and your friend, um, Sharon is it?"

"People call me Sid now," said Sid with a forced smile and a little wave. "Hi." She had never liked the self-assured jerk. The high school jock had been a spoiled brat all the way through school. His family owned a neighboring vineyard to Charity's family's land. For some reason Charity had had a crush on him when they were in junior high. She said he was her reserve dream man in case Brick fell through. Remembering that made Sid shudder. She felt trouble and her intuitions were rarely wrong.

"Yes, Sid and I were just catching up. I was about to leave when I neglected to look where I was going, as usual. Sorry."

"Are you on your way out? I'd love to walk you to your car." Charity looked at him. Something about him had changed. He was more grown up, but the overconfidence that came from being the star athlete was still showing.

"Sure, why not, although I'm perfectly capable of taking care of myself. I don't need a man to walk me to a well-lit parking spot in front of the building."

"Well, you haven't changed much, Charity Henley. Still sassy as ever." He laughed, put his arm around her shoulders, and led her to the door.

Sid was left alone to consider what had just happened. Tucker was trouble, or he always had been. The high school quarterback and prom king had always gotten what he wanted, and at the moment it looked like that was Charity. Sid decided to give it five minutes before she sent a text to Charity, then she was out that door to see what was going on.

The man rose from his booth to approach her, but as soon as he did, Charity collided with Tucker Morrison. "Damn," he said under his breath. He had missed his chance, but he followed with his head down to see where they were going.

Chapter Five

Charity's car was literally a few steps outside the front door. That's life in a small town. Tucker still kept a protective arm at her waist. He had learned long ago that women seemed to like that, even someone as strong-willed as Charity Henley. The halogen light on the lamp post cast a warm, orange glow over them, creating a romantic feeling that Tucker was hoping she would pick up on.

It was difficult for the man to follow them out without being seen. He pulled his hat lower over his forehead and looked down at the ground, but they were busy reminiscing about old times and didn't seem to notice him. He stepped around the corner of the building and watched from the shadows. He'd always been good about blending in with his surroundings. It had served him well over the years.

"So, what are your plans, now that college is behind you?" asked Tucker.

"I'm going to be working for my father, as head of marketing and research." It was the first time Charity had said it out loud to anyone other than Sid, and she liked the way it sounded.

"Congratulations," said Tucker with a small salute. "That's a nice gig."

"And you?"

"I've been trying to separate myself from my father's vineyard. I'm tired of the grape and wine business. I'm thinking of buying The Duck. That's why I was here tonight."

"Wow! You, the owner of The Painted Duck? Now that's something I hadn't ever imagined." Charity was surprised. She always thought of Tucker as being someone who would ride the wave of his parents' wealth once his hoped-for career as a pro football player had gone nowhere.

"Why are you so surprised?

"No reason," she laughed, "except that might mean that you would actually have to work for a living."

"Aw, Charity, that was low. I've grown up just like you have. And boy, have you ever, all curves and softness now." He moved in closer, and Charity allowed it for a moment to see where he was going. His arm tightened around her waist bringing her in as he leaned in for a gentle kiss. She let it happen. 'Nice,' she thought, 'but no fireworks.'

The man's fist tightened into a ball as he watched from around the corner. He could feel his heart rate escalate.

Charity pulled back, as he pressed a little firmer. "Whoa, Tucker, where is this coming from?"

"It's been so good seeing you again. I couldn't help myself. And it's not exactly the first time we've kissed. We were quite an item for a while in high school, remember? We could have gone somewhere together."

"Yes. I remember the whole prom king-and-queen thing. But as I recall it, you were all hands, and I wasn't ready for that. And I'm still not, not right now anyway. I've got a new career on my mind." She pushed him gently back.

"No time for dating, then?" He pouted in an exaggerated way.

"Maybe, but whatever I decide, I want you to know, right up front, that I'm not looking for anything serious. I could agree to some fun times, but I will never allow myself to get serious, not with anyone."

"Fun times sounds good to me. Can I call you soon? You never know. I might be able to change your mind," he said in a low growl. He pulled her in tighter, and this time the kiss was anything but gentle. He pulled back, leaving Charity breathless. "You'll be hearing from me real soon, Charity Henley." And he walked away leaving her dizzy and wondering what in the world had just happened. She put her key in the car with shaky fingers and drove away, still trying to sort it all out.

The man in the shadows was breathing heavily. It had been painful to watch. 'Why had she let that happen?' he wondered. 'Didn't she realize what kind of man Tucker Morrison was?' Now that he was sure she was in her car and away from the clutches of that jerk, he got in his own car, and followed her at a safe distance. He was relieved when she turned into her driveway, unharmed. There was still a chance for him to approach her, maybe tomorrow. He needed to declare his intentions. She was his – she had always been his.

Charity parked her car by the front porch and sat there a moment. She still wasn't sure what to think about Tucker kissing her. It's not like they hadn't kissed before, but this time was different. He was a man now, and it was obvious he wanted more from her than a few kisses, but she was not about to be his one-night stand. She would be no man's play toy. Her cell phone buzzed, startling her from her thoughts.

"Charity, are you okay?" It was just Sid checking in.

"Sure, I'm fine. I'm home now." It was good to know that she had such a caring friend.

"Oh good, I wasn't sure what Tucker had in mind, there. You know I never trusted him. And when I went outside to check on you, you were gone."

"Yeah – sure—but everything's good. He did ask me out, though, but I told him I had to think about it."

"Oh, Charity, don't go there, especially on a rebound of sorts from Brick. That could be real trouble."

"Don't worry about me. I know what I'm doing. Maybe we'll just have some fun dating. That's all. I told him I wasn't looking for anything serious."

"Well, be careful. You just got back into town. There are lot of fish out there, but, in my opinion, I consider Tucker Morrison to be a dangerous shark."

"Warning heeded. Thank you, ma'am. 'Night, Sid. We'll talk tomorrow."

"I'm counting on it. Goodnight."

Charity saw her mother peek out through the curtains, still counting her chickens -- a habit she would probably never give up. She laughed and went inside, being careful not to let the screen door bang behind her. She headed up the stairs to get her much needed sleep. Tomorrow was a new day; she was looking forward to starting her new position at Diamante Vineyard.

Instead of the sunshine that was predicted, morning brought an overcast, grey day along with the kind of cold, rainy drizzle that could go straight to your bones. Charity looked out the window from her second-story bedroom. This would not be the best day to walk the vineyard rows and check out what stage the grapes were at. She was disappointed. She had wanted to be able to have a conversation with the staff and field workers. She was hoping to show them that she had some knowledge of growing grapes, since she had grown up on the farm. The truth is, that even though she had followed her father around when she was small, and he was always telling her about the ways to prune the vines, and how to look out for insects like the Japanese beetle or the grape berry moth, she really hadn't absorbed all that much. She knew that certain diseases could devastate a crop if not controlled, such as powdery mildew, downy mildew, and black rot. Charity had heard discussions around the table about such things all her life, but to be honest, she always figured the men could handle the problems, and at that age she was definitely against taking any part in the wine business. She just enjoyed following her father around and spending time with him. She knew the real talent was her brother, Trey. He had just as much, or more, knowledge than her father about the grape and wine industry. He was to be the shining star and future manager of the land. But then he had gone off and joined the Marines, a shock to them all. It was wonderful that he was back, but he seemed to have more on his mind and had lost all interest in grapes.

Now that she was an adult, Charity still had no interest in learning the details of farm life, but she knew she would need to know something about the daily operations in order to gain respect. Apparently, today was not to be the day to learn how to fight beetles and moths.

Since the day had turned out to be gloomy, she dressed in jeans, thick socks with her muck boots, and then pulled on a warm fleece hoodie over her tee shirt. She grabbed a cup of hot black coffee and took a bite of toast and then headed out the door. She had decided the best course for today would be to tour the out buildings. She could dodge the raindrops by running from her car to each barn and maybe meet a few people inside. The migrant workers came and went, but there were a few who had been employed here for many years. The trusted crew bosses were the ones who hired and fired the transient workers, and they were responsible for keeping the interior of the buildings clean, organized, and functioning, so on a rainy day like this, she knew she could find them indoors.

Charity took the dirt drive across their property to the other side of the vines to a barn they called the machinery barn. It held tractors, trucks, and flatbeds, and there was usually someone working on an engine or greasing some part. She parked as close to the door as possible, then ran in, letting the door bang loudly behind her. A man looked up from his work at the workbench with a startled look on his face, until he recognized the pretty young woman; then his face lit up like a neon sign. "Charity, so nice to see you."

"Hi, Mateo," she quickly stepped forward to give him a hug. "Oh, forgive me. I forgot about my wet clothes."

"Not a problem. It's just water," he said. "I'm sorry I couldn't make it to your party. My mother has not been doing well, so we've had to put her in a nursing home. She's not adjusting as we had hoped.

So I've been spending a lot of my free time with her until she makes new friends."

"Oh that's too bad. She must be in her eighties by now, right?"

"Yes, she's 84, and she's basically healthy, but frail, and unable to care for herself any longer. I'm hoping she gets used to her new surroundings soon. It's hard to leave your home when you're old."

"I can imagine. Please, the next time you see her, give her my best."

"So," he said with a grin, "I heard something about you staying on and working with your dad and brother."

"Yes, I'm to be the new head of marketing and research. I'll oversee advertising and brand awareness. So don't worry," she laughed, "I won't get in your hair."

"You know I think of you fondly. You could never get in my hair," said the older man, patting her shoulder.

"Thanks, Mateo. You've been around here since I was a baby; maybe longer. You were always there for me whenever I skinned a knee or got a cut and I was afraid to tell my parents what I'd been doing. And I'm sure my father could not get along without you." She hugged him again, this time a little tighter. "Enough of this love fest. I want to make the rounds of all of the buildings and then go set up my office. I can see there's not a lot I need to know here, but I'll be back soon. Maybe we can have a cup of coffee together on your break."

"Sounds good, chiquita, and congratulations on your new job."

Charity ran back out to the car. It was pouring out now; she was drenched by the time she got back in the car.

Her next stop was the old, empty, wooden barn. Most of the other buildings were what were called pole barns. They were an all-steel structure and were made to last with very little upkeep; they had changed the landscape of the rolling hills of Michigan. Taking pictures of old barns had become a passion for those who were afraid of losing them forever. As each antique barn fell, due to weather or disrepair, a new steel pole building was erected. Charity loved that they still had a real barn on the property; as it stated above the door, it had been erected in 1875. It was massive, and the stain had faded to a rusty red color, just as old barns should, she thought. She wanted to stop there next and check out the possibilities, and if she could convince her father of it, this would be her first project.

This barn sat quite a ways from the machinery barn, because it had been on the property when her parents had purchased the land. The other out buildings had been placed in their positions for convenience, but her father had not wanted this one taken down, so it was at the end of a lane rarely used and most probably near the original farm house. Charity sat in her car and looked up at the peak of the roof. She imagined how just a few years after the end of the Civil War this barn would have been erected.

Maybe neighbors and friends had come together for a barn raising. Perhaps a new family was about to set up their homestead here. She could practically hear the sounds of pounding hammers while men called to each other with coordinating instructions, each one knowing exactly what they were supposed to do because they had done it so many times before. Maybe the children were running and playing on the grounds; the girls shrieking as the boys chased them with snakes and toads. She was sure the women would have set long tables under one of the huge oak trees, and they would walk back and forth to their nearby buggies as they carried food in gingham-covered baskets for the afternoon meal that they had prepared at home. Barns were the heart and soul of a farm. Without one, a farmer could not keep his livestock warm and dry from the weather or store his newly harvested crop until taking it to market. Buggies, horses, tack, cows, straw, and hay were also kept in the barns. Barns were the lifeblood of the family. Spencer Henley had always insisted that his barn be kept in repair. He loved that old building about as much as Charity did.

A clap of thunder almost sent Charity through the roof of her car. She had always hated thunderstorms, and preferred to be safely inside, especially during lightning. Now that she was jarred out of her daydreaming, she decided to make a dash for the door, before any lightning bolts headed her way. She noticed the padlock, hanging open on its bracket. Her father would be very upset if he knew about this lack of attention. Someone had missed checking the lock on their nightly rounds. She would need to point that omission out to her dad.

A gust of wind seemed to push her car sideways, as the strength of the storm began to build. She forced the door open and made a run to the barn door. With a lot of effort, she was able to slide it sideways just enough for her to slip inside. The smell of the dirt floor and the old wood brought her back to her childhood. It had been her favorite place to hide as a child. She would climb the wooden steps to the loft with her book in hand and read all afternoon. She had even secretly left her sleeping bag behind on one trip, and then when it was needed for a camping trip, she had told her mother she couldn't find it, so they had had to buy her a new one. She had carried different items up there a little at a time so her parents wouldn't notice they were missing. Eventually, she had set up her very own hideout, complete with a box for her dolls and books, a flashlight, some matches, and finally she had been able to confiscate a lantern and some oil. She had never found use for the flashlight or lamp when she was young, because she wasn't allowed to be outside after dark, but during her tumultuous teen years, this place had been her sanctuary. It had been the place where she and – no, she shook her head. She didn't want to go there. It was best forgotten.

Suddenly, her eye caught a movement in the back of the barn. She moved slowly forward to one of the stalls where old wine barrels had been stored in recent years. Holding her breath and not knowing what she would find, animal or man, she picked up an antique pitchfork that had been left leaning against a wall. She slowly worked her way to the opening of the stall, where she discovered a man with his back to her, looking over the barrels. He was completely unaware of her presence. She relaxed a bit when she recognized his profile. He hadn't changed much over the years; her heart began to race. 'Don't be silly,' she scolded herself. She stood very still as she observed his familiar movements. His back was broader now and he seemed a few inches taller than the last time she had seen him. His shoulders were more muscular and his biceps bulged at the end of the short sleeve of his black tee; his muscles seemed to move on their own volition as he bent over the barrels, running his hands over them, checking each one by touch, as gentle as if he were caressing a woman. His jeans were tight-fitting; she took a moment to appreciate the view. She was breathing faster now, and almost felt faint. 'What's wrong with me,' she wondered. He turned suddenly as soon as he felt her watching him. They had always had a connection that way; he could sense her and she him, across time and space. He popped his earbuds out and a slow, sexy smile spread across his face.

"Well, look what the cat dragged in. A soggy wet mouse." He chuckled with the joy of seeing her here in this barn again. It was more than he had hoped for.

"Hello Gabe. How have you been? I was wondering when we would run into each other again. I didn't realize you were home, too." Charity felt shaky. Why? It was just her old friend Gabe – Gabriel Rivera, Mateo's son, her schoolmate and friend. Yes, her friend, that's all he was; Charity tossed her head to clear out long-buried memories.

He reached for his red plaid shirt, pulled it on, leaving it hang loosely open; she remembered it was the way he had always preferred wearing his shirts. His ball cap sat low over his eyes, but she could feel them roaming slowly over her body. They had not left each other on good terms the last time they were together, and she wasn't sure how she would be received. He waited a moment before he responded. He loved gazing at the vision of her. She was finally back. He breathed a big sigh of relief. The last few years had been agony without her.

"Well, actually," he finally answered, "I never left. I've always been here. I stayed out of your way whenever you came home on break; I found things to do and places to go -- so you wouldn't have to look at me again," he said softly.

She began to shiver; he noticed her shaking, thinking it was fear. He was ashamed. He decided this was not the time to mention that he had seen her at The Painted Duck with Tucker Morrison. Skulking in the shadows while spying on her and Tucker had not been his finest moment.

Suddenly, Gabe realized how wet she actually was. Her hair was dripping as if she were just out of a shower. And although the image that brought to mind was very pleasing to him, he could see her discomfort.

"You're freezing. Here, sit over by the stove in the old tack room. I'll get a fire started."

He hurried to grab a small crate close by and carried it next to the wood burning, pot-belly stove, that had been installed just in case someone ever got trapped here in the winter. Then he moved forward and led her by the elbow. It felt so good to touch her again. He thought he felt her pull back slightly, but then she allowed him the privilege of guiding her. Her shivering was uncontrollable now, but she refused to sit down. He quickly grabbed some pieces of wood from the nearby emergency stack, reached in his pocket for a match, and after banking the stove with kindling which had been left at the ready, he lit the fire.

"You need to get this hoodie off. It's soaked," he said huskily. He began to pull it off, himself, but she rejected him.

"I can do it." Charity shot him a glare. She unzipped the hoodie, and he could see that her tee shirt was soaked through, also. He knew she was cold and miserable, but he was enjoying what he saw. There was a time she would not have minded if he had helped her. But too much had been said between them, things that could not be taken back.

He opened a cupboard and pulled out a freshly cleaned afghan that he had just placed there today. She looked at him in surprise. "We always keep some supplies here now, since one of the field hands was trapped here in a blizzard a few years ago. Your dad put me on that detail. Look, a few cans of food, a can opener, some bottled water, matches, and flashlights. There's even a hand-crank radio." He heard himself rambling, not like him at all. He was usually the quiet one, while she had been the happy, joyful girl. He remembered how she had love to dance, twirling and laughing, while he preferred to watch. She sang while he played his guitar. They had their Mexican heritage with their dark hair and eyes in common, but her genes were part German, bringing an exotic look to her features that made her quite different than most.

They were yin and yang, and therefore, in his mind, they were perfect for each other.

He tried once again to get close enough to her in order to place the afghan around her shoulders, but she yanked it from his hands. "Why are you here? In this building, I mean." She softened her voice so as not to sound so confrontational. "And what were you doing back there?" She was hoping to get the conversation back on a more casual footing.

"I was taking inventory. We need to figure out how many extra barrels we have that are usable. It's a long way 'til harvest, but we're planning ahead. Some of these have been in here for a long time." He stopped a moment and decided to forge ahead. He had something to say that needed saying. "Tee, I'm sorry for -- "

"I haven't been called that in a very long time," said Charity, softly. "You were the only one who ever did." She smiled slightly.

He saw her relax a little; maybe it was the heat from the fire, or maybe she was warming up to him.

Gabe felt now that he had broken the ice, he could try to push forward with his speech. He had rehearsed it over and over in preparation for the next time he saw her. "I've been wanting to tell you for the last two years how sorry I am for how we ended. I was wrong to say what I did. I never meant to hurt you." He looked down and then back up to see how she responded to what he said.

Charity noticed some tears well up in his eyes. She couldn't bear it. It had all been her fault, after all. He had only told her the truth; it was a truth she couldn't bear to hear at that time.

"It's all good, Gabe. I've grown up a lot since then. I've had to take a long hard look at myself recently, and I wasn't happy with what I discovered. So, I'll agree that you were right, but it doesn't mean I like how you handled it. Anyway, I've tried my best to make changes. I know now for certain that Brick will never be a part of my life, and he was never meant to be. He was always meant for Belle. I figured that out a few days ago, when they announced that they are going to have a baby. I have to get rid of that pipedream once and for all."

Gabe had been holding his breath. He slowly let it out so she would not see his relief. He turned his head slightly, swallowed the lump in his throat, and swiped at a tear that had escaped even though he had willed it to stay put. "That's great, Tee. I'm happy for you. But what does that mean for us?" he asked hopefully.

"The same as always, Gabe. Friends. I'm not interested in anything else. I'm done with men, and I've sworn against marriage. If you can handle friendship only, we can go back to the way things were before – "

She felt her face flush to the color of a beet.

"Tee, I'll take you any way I can get you, you know that. I want you in my life, that's all."

"Okay, then. Let's move forward and never look back. Deal?"

"Deal."

She meant to shake his hand as she had her father's, but one look in his eyes, and she was drawn in for a hug. She felt tears sting her eyes. 'What is wrong with me,' she wondered again.

Over her shoulder, Gabe closed his eyes and thanked God for her return to his life. The hug lasted a little longer and was slightly tighter than the friendship code called for, and he relished in it. She was back home. His Tee was back.

Chapter Six

In those few short moments in Gabe's arms, Charity had felt like she was truly home. Gabe had always been her safety net, her comfort, and her joy. He had been her sanctuary, as much as the loft itself, especially through her senior year of high school. Gabe and the loft went hand in hand. But now things were different. She was trying to be a new person; one who no longer relied on a man to get her through tough times. She stiffened, pulled back, and went to sit by the stove. The warmth relaxed her a bit. She felt a little more comfortable with him now. She was in control of the situation; she was sure of it.

Gabe felt the awkward silence and tried to move the conversation toward a new topic. "Tell me why you're here – in the barn, I mean." he asked.

She looked into his deep brown eyes, getting lost for a moment. He was always so interested in everything about her. Then she cleared her throat and said, "I have an idea about turning this barn into a place for rustic weddings and other types of celebrations, like special anniversaries or graduations. I've looked at a lot of books and magazines, and barn weddings seem to be the thing lately. We're lucky to have such a solid old barn, and I thought we could use it as one more way to promote our brand."

"What do you mean by that?" He loved watching her talk; he could ask questions all day long just to keep her going. Her smooth skin was perfection; he yearned to reach out and touch her face, feel the softness he remembered. Her hands were expressive; he wanted to hold them, caress her lovely fingers, and kiss her palms.

"Well," she said, excited to explain it to someone, "I want to build a bar that will serve only our label. I thought about stringing Edison lights all over. Maybe I'll have an indoor arch or gazebo built that the bride and groom can stand under to get married. I can envision tables with white cloths, glowing lights, and flowers on each one of them. The place should sparkle, but still keep the integrity of an old building, with the wood plank floors and massive beams. There could be some old lanterns and other antiques sitting around and hanging on the walls. The guests can watch the wedding from their tables and then just keep their seats for the meal later, if it's catered."

"I think that might go over big, here," he commented. "What about restroom facilities, though? Right now, we just have an outhouse."

"Yes, I've thought of that; that's something I would need a builder to help me with. I'm hoping to get an estimate on plumbing, and of course, the place will have to be inspected to make sure it's safe for the public."

"It might work, though. There's already water wells in several areas nearby to supply the irrigation system. You could tap into one of those. But you'll need a septic system, and that could be costly."

"I hadn't thought about a septic tank. Well, those are things I need to discuss with my father. I'll call and get estimates first thing tomorrow."

Charity had forgotten how easy the flow of their conversation had always been. If Gabe would agree to her request of friendship only, she would be happy to return to the way things were – before senior year, that is.

Gabe stood to throw more wood on the fire. Charity watched his panther-like movements, shook her head to clear images of the past, and said, "Don't bother – unless you're planning to stay a while. I have to go. I'm dried off, and it sounds like the rain has let up." She stood up, then stretched to get her hoodie from a hook on the wall above her head where Gabe had hung it. "Oh, this feels good. Warm and dry."

Gabe stepped forward to help her reach it, although she didn't really need him to get it down. He gently placed his hands on her shoulders to remove the afghan, turned her toward him, then he slid his hands down her arms to rest on her hands. He enclosed her fingers in his. They stood closely, looking deeply into each other's eyes, trying to decide what the next move was to be. Gabe moved forward, forcing Charity to move back. She had no fear, never with Gabe, but she wasn't sure how she would ever keep her resolve for just friendship if he kept doing things like this. She felt herself bump into a wall. There was nowhere to go; he continued one more step until his body was touching hers. Then he slowly raised her arms above her head and pinned them to the wall, as he leaned in for the kiss he had been waiting for since she had left him over two years ago.

Charity gave in; she had lost all control, now. Whenever she was with Gabe, it was all about raw emotion, but this time the kiss was sweet, and tender, and as he relaxed his hands to move down her body, she responded by wrapping her arms around his neck. She ran her fingers through his hair -- his thick, luscious, dark hair. She was breathing heavier now because she knew where this was going. Soon she wouldn't be able to stop herself; she would reach a point of no return. "Gabe, oh Gabe," she said with her lips still on his. "Please, no. Let's don't do this. Please." She felt weak in the knees, almost hoping he would continue, so when he stopped as she had requested, while looking at her intensely, she felt a mixture of relief and disappointment. He pulled her head to his chest, and whispered, "One of these days, Tee, you're finally going to figure out who it is that you want, and I plan to be the one you choose. I want that man to be me; it's what I've always wanted, what I've prayed for, since we were kids. We belong together, and deep down you know it. So I can't promise I won't try this again."

With one more, gentle kiss on the lips, he placed his hat on his head, turned, and left the barn. Charity had not seen a car, so she could only assume he was walking back to the winery in the rain. She was stunned by what had just taken place. 'Gabe, Gabe,' she thought, 'why do you always complicate things for me?' She tossed some water on the fire, took one last look at the barn, and wondered if she would be able to continue with her plans with him on the premises.

Charity spent the rest of the afternoon organizing the office space her father had set aside for her. He had thoughtfully had one of the men set up a desk with a laptop computer which was there waiting for her work to begin. A new printer had been placed on a table in the corner, ready for the graphs and charts she would have to produce in order to convince him she was making the right decisions. She had always enjoyed this type of activity. She loved paper and pens and notebooks and folders. Trips to office supply stores were some of her favorite outings when she was young. Now of course, the shopping list also included, printer paper, flash drives, and ink cartridges. She kept as busy as possible in order to block out what had occurred at the barn, but flashes of Gabe's face kept coming to the surface of her mind. Brick was the man she had wanted for most of her life, so she couldn't understand the magnetic pull toward Gabe whenever she was near him.

It hadn't always been that way. They used to play as children do, with no recognition of the fact that they were different – boy and girl. She remembered how they would play 'house,' pretending to be husband and wife. Charity had learned to make a gum wrapper ring in school, so she put it on the fourth finger of her left hand, whenever they played this game. In her child's mind, it mimicked her mother's wedding ring. He would pretend to go off to work in the grapes, and she pretended to cook his meal by making mud pies and serving him 'coffee' in her tea set.

Then one day, when they were about 12, and the childish games were long behind them, they were running across a field, when Gabe grabbed her hand, as he had done so many times before. But this time, when they stopped to catch their breath, there was an awkwardness that they hadn't felt before. He dropped her hand, and they pretended not to notice that anything had changed.

Not more than a week later, they were sitting on the bank of a small stream, called Owl Creek, which ran behind the house in a wooded area. It was a hot summer day, so they had been wading, and they were now sitting side by side in order to dry their feet before putting their shoes back on. Charity and Gabe were laughing at something hysterically. Charity had the giggles and couldn't seem to stop. Suddenly, Gabe learned over and kissed her, in the immature way of a first kiss. It was no more than a quick peck at first. Charity remembered how startled she had been, but she did like it, so she let him try once more, this time the connection lasted a little longer. When they pulled apart, they were both embarrassed at what had occurred, so they never said a word about it for quite some time.

A month or so later, they were watching the fireworks that the neighboring farmer was shooting off in his field. It was very dark, other than the sparkling colors in the sky. The adults were busy chatting with each other on the porch; the crickets and tree frogs were temporarily silent, as the noise and flashing lights had scared them back to wherever insects and amphibians go to hide. No one seemed to notice that the two pre-teens had slipped away to the side of the house where it was dark and shielded from parental vision. Gabe caught her hand and pulled her in for what was to be one of their many kisses from that day on. Charity never even told Sid about what she and Gabe had been doing. She didn't know why. She had just wanted to keep it private. And she was embarrassed about the fact that all she talked about was how Brick was supposed to be the man of her dreams, and here she was, enjoying Gabe's kisses – enjoying them very much, in fact. It was confusing to her then, and it was confusing now. Yes, she was done with Brick, she was certain of it. But what about that kiss with Tucker? She had liked that, too, although she hadn't felt sparks and tingles like she always felt with Gabe. Was she bound to be one of those women that others whispered about? Going from man to man for self-gratification? She would not allow that to happen to her. That was the reason why she had sworn off men. Apparently, she was just too weak to be around them.

Charity brushed the hair behind her ear. It was straight and shiny like her mother's. She was glad she had inherited that feature from her. But she had also inherited her short stature. She wished she had been a little taller than her five foot two, but even though Gabe was taller than the average Mexican-American male, they had fit together very well. 'No, no!' she screamed in her head. 'I won't let myself go there.'

"No" she said out loud as she bent over to pick up a paperclip that had fallen on the floor.

"Is there a problem? Can I help?"

Charity was so startled that she stood up quickly and hit her head on the edge of the desk. "Ouch!" She put her hand to her head, turned, and looked straight at Tucker Morrison leaning casually against the door jamb.

Tucker was one of those guys that women found attractive at first glance. He was tall with sandy hair; he had eyes that changed from green to blue depending on what he was wearing, captivating most women almost instantly. His athletic build, which had done him well in the female department, had failed him on the football field. Both his high school and college career were spectacular, but for some reason he was never able to make the transition to pro ball successfully. Rumor had it that his competitive father was extremely disappointed. He had spent many years of Tucker's youth bragging about his son, and now he had had to eat his words.

Tucker's slow smile spread across his handsome face. "Sorry, I didn't mean to startle you."

"Oh, hi, Tuck. I was just uh – retrieving a paperclip." Charity stood up quickly, smoothing a few wisps of hair which had escaped while she had been hanging upside down. "Nice to see you again. What can I do for you?"

"I just thought I would stop by and see how you were getting along with your new job. One of the guys out front pointed the way to your office. Nice digs."

"I'm just getting settled in, but thank you. Would you like to sit down? You're my first visitor."

"Thanks, but I can't stay. I'm on an urgent errand, apparently, for Dad. He always seems to be in a rush, but I wanted to stop by and ask if you would like to go out with me for dinner?"

"Oh – uh – you caught me off-guard. I -- uh, yes, I guess I could." Charity had no idea why she had said yes. She had just pushed Gabe away, and now she was accepting a date with Tucker. 'I'm a crazy mess,' she thought, 'that's for sure.'

Tucker's smile got bigger. "Tonight? Seven o'clock? The Duck?"

"Okay, I'll meet you there. It'll be nice to catch up and talk about the old gang."

"Yes, yes it will," he said. "See you later, then."

She watched as Tucker walked through the winery, talking to the workers as he went. It seemed as though everyone knew him, and they were more than happy to take time from their day to chat. He showed no sign of being rushed to get to an errand for his father.

"Hmm, that's strange," said Charity out loud, then caught herself by saying, "I've got to stop talking to myself."

Chapter Seven

Getting ready for her date that evening, and planning her outfit was more challenging than normal. She had neglected to ask Tucker what side of The Painted Duck they would be eating in. The Duck had a dress code for the fine dining side, but the only dress requirement on the bar side was a sign that said 'no shirt, no shoes, no service.' It was amazing how many beachgoers from out of state thought they could pop in for a burger in their bathing suits and bare feet. So jeans and tee shirts were okay there, but on the 'fancy side,' as the locals called it, jeans, shorts, and flip-flops were not allowed. It was a minor dilemma that Charity could easily solve. She had a large wardrobe that included a variety of clothing for all types of weather and occasions. And of course, the perfect shoes were always close at hand – her daddy had seen to it.

She finally settled on a nice pair of slacks, a thin, crocheted, short-sleeved sweater that clung closely to her body, and wedged sandals. Although the days were warmer and summer was fast approaching, the evenings could still get quite cool, so she took along a light jacket to toss in the car. She tied her long dark hair up in a high ponytail, and with some new dangling earrings she had just received from her Tia Rosa for graduation, she was the perfect combination of casual and dressy. Just right for her 'sort-of-date,' as she had described it to her mother. She grabbed her purse, made sure the car keys and cell phone were still in it, and after kissing her mother goodbye and giving her brother Trey a quick wave, she went out the door.

A frown creased Trey's forehead. He turned to their mother and said, "I wonder what that date is all about? Why Tucker?"

"She's still young, and of course, very beautiful. You know how it is; you date this one and then you date that one, trying to find the perfect life partner. It's almost like a game, but with higher stakes."

"Yeah, but I'm never sure when it comes to Tucker what kind of game he's playing."

"Keep an eye on things, will you Trey? And by that, I don't mean follow her around. Just keep your listening ears open. Okay? Don't encroach on her privacy."

"Got it, Mom. Does Dad know?"

"I haven't mentioned it; I'm waiting and watching. No sense in stirring things up."

Charity pulled her yellow Mustang off the driveway and onto the highway that led to town. She hadn't paid much attention to the green car behind her; she had just gauged the distance of the oncoming headlights to make sure she had enough clearance to pull out in front of it. Soon the car was close to her rear bumper, but because of the dark, she was completely unaware that she was in front of Gabe's car. Gabe had no problem identifying her bright sports car. It had not been his intention to follow Charity; it was just a stroke of luck that he had arrived at her driveway at that exact moment. He had almost thought about flashing his lights at her as a sign of hello, but then realized that she might take it as a sign of trouble. He stayed a respectable distance behind her, and as they approached Main Street, he dropped back even further. He didn't want her to think that he had followed her intentionally.

Gabe was stopped at a stoplight when Charity pulled into a parking spot in front of The Painted Duck. He assumed she was meeting Sid again, until he noticed Tucker Morrison's blue Corvette. His heart skipped a beat. Could she be going on a date with him? He hadn't liked the way Tucker had come on to her the other night, and Gabe had heard talk around the winery that Tucker had been on the property earlier today. The stoplight turned green, and since there were no cars behind him, he was able to drive slowly by the restaurant. He looked for Sid's copper HHR;

no sign of it. 'Maybe she's late, or Charity's early,' he thought. 'No, Sid is never late to anything and Charity is never early.' He decided to drive around back to the parking lot in the rear, but still he found no other recognizable car. He hit his palm on the steering wheel in frustration. He knew without a shadow of a doubt that she was in there with him. He also knew that, just like always, he would never be able to compete with the guy who had everything -- money, good looks, charisma, and local fame.

This wasn't what he had planned for this evening, but he decided it was worth it to cancel out on meeting the guys for their weekly poker night. They wouldn't be happy, but they'd have to deal with it. This was far more important.

After selecting a parking spot and locking the car, he walked in the back door to the bar. He had decided to sit in his corner spot, if it was available, and nurse a beer while watching the front door; that way he could tell if she left with Tucker or if she had met someone else, and he wouldn't look like a fool trying to peek in the dining area.

Charity and Tucker were seated when Gabe walked in, and the server was offering them something to drink. They were in a lively discussion as to which wine label they would select. Since they were from competing families, they finally decided on a Sonny Rosso wine for dinner and a Diamante wine for dessert.

Charity was searching for something to talk about. She had not known Tucker extremely well, other than at school. Being on the football team had kept him busy in high school with practices and games, but since she was a cheerleader, and the school was small, they had hung around with the same crowd. They casually dated for a few months, and suddenly everyone expected them to be an item. It was a complete shock to them both when they were voted homecoming king and queen. At that point in her life,

Charity was very confused about Brick. She had discovered the summer before her senior year that Brick was in love with her newly found sister. She was so devastated that dating anyone seriously seemed out of the question. But then there was Gabe – her secret, her shame, her – she didn't know what he was. She felt herself redden at the memory, and rather than let Tucker see her discomfort, she quickly asked a question to keep him talking.

"Tuck, I never knew where the name for your family's label came from. What, or who, does Sonny Rosso represent?"

Tucker looked pleased to find something to talk to Charity about. The conversation had been a little stilted up to now, but wineries were common ground, and a subject he had fully intended to bring up anyway.

"Well, I'm not sure if you're aware, but my mother's family is of Italian descent."

"Oh, no, I didn't know. With a last name of Morrison, I wouldn't have guessed that." She took a sip of Sonny Rosso chardonnay which the server had placed in front of her. She had to admit, it was very good.

"Yes, my mother's family is the Rosso name; they came to America many years ago, and settled in northern Michigan. Who knows why, but I guess they saw something in the elevation, the rolling hills, and the nearness of the lake that encouraged them to believe they could grow grapes, and they were right. For two generations they were grape growers. They were nothing more than the farmer that produced grapes for grape juice companies, but then wineries began to purchase their grapes, and their business really thrived. When my Dad met and married my mother, they lived on the farm with her parents, and he learned everything he could about the grape business. He saw the potential for more; he wanted to produce quality wines, but my grandfather didn't want any part of it. Grandpa said he felt safe doing what he knew and didn't want to take a risk."

"I can understand that," added Charity. "Growing grapes is risky enough without adding to the demands of making wine."

"Yes, well, he wouldn't budge, but after he passed away, my mother and father decided to start making wine like they had long dreamed about doing. They wanted to use the Rosso name, but it was already taken, so they added Sonny which is what my father was called when he was young – taken from the last syllable in Morrison. They felt that Sonny sounded like sunny, spelled with a U, and thought people would be drawn to it. From that they created a purple sun for the label, and the rest is history."

"Very interesting story," said Charity with a smile, "and so we find ourselves neighbors and competitors."

"Friendly competitors, right?" He reached over to take her hand. She allowed it for a second and then pulled back, making a move to wipe her mouth with her napkin.

"Okay, then," said Tucker feeling the slight rebuff, "let's look at our menus, before the waiter comes back."

The rest of the meal was filled with chit chat about old friends. Charity asked who was still living in Frankfort and who had moved away. They talked about marriages, divorces, and who of their old friends had children. It was more of an old home week than a romantic dinner, and for that, Charity was relieved.

Their meal was fabulous and Charity was stuffed, but Tucker insisted on dessert. He wasn't ready to let her go yet. He ordered a black cherry mud pie for them to share, and he asked her to choose her favorite dessert wine to pair with it. She selected a Riesling from Diamante called Lighthouse. It carried notes of honey that would be perfect with the chocolate. After their first taste, Tucker complimented her on her choice and then they began eating off of the same plate with two spoons. Charity hadn't been sure about that idea. It seemed too intimate, and she was nowhere near to being ready for any type of intimacy.

"So, Tucker, tell me about your idea of buying The Duck. I didn't realize it was for sale."

"It isn't really. I've been working on the owner, Duane, to cut me a deal. I think he's getting ready to retire."

Charity noticed that Tucker's body language had changed. His face lit up, and he seemed charged with energy.

"What made you want to buy a restaurant and bar? You'll most likely inherit Sonny Rosso, won't you?"

"Yeah, I will. But I've never been a fan of growing grapes. Dad had a hard time getting me to work in the fields when I was young. He wanted me to learn the business from the ground up, but I strongly objected, so he skipped to the winery and tried to teach me how to make wine. I didn't care for that, either. Besides I thought I was going to be a pro football player." He chuckled with a wry smile; Charity could see that he felt that he had failed his father on both counts.

"I can relate," she said. "There was a time that I rebelled against it, too. Actually, I rebelled against everything that had to do with my family. But I came around – or maybe I'm still a work in progress. But I'm trying, anyway."

"I had other dreams, dreams that my father would not have understood at that point."

"Really? What was that?"

Now he had her interest. "I wanted to be a chef, but when I tried to tell Dad, he said no son of his was going to cook in the kitchen. He said 'Stick to football. It's a man's game.' "

Charity was surprised but tried not to let it show on her face. She could see that Tucker was serious and didn't want to hurt his feelings. "That doesn't seem to fit your image, but I believe that you should always follow your heart. So what's next for you?"

"Dad finally came around, and agreed to finance my purchase, if I'd carry our label exclusively."

"Oh." Charity couldn't help but let the disappointment show on her face.

"Did I say something wrong?" asked Tucker.

"No, not at all." She would not let him know that was part of her strategy for Diamante Wines. She had planned to present it to her father tomorrow. Well, she'd have to make a change of direction until she heard how things worked out with Tucker's idea to purchase The Duck.

"Well, good luck to you. I hope it all works out for you." She glanced at the large Howard Miller clock on the wall. "You know, it's really getting late, and I should be going."

"So soon?" He was not ready to let her go yet. He had more to accomplish. "I thought we could take a walk on the pier and head out to the lighthouse to watch the sunset."

"Okay," she said reluctantly. "But just part way out. It'll be getting damp and chilly near the water by now. Let's both move our cars over there, and then we can leave for home from that point."

"Sounds like a plan. You go ahead. I'll get the bill."

"See you in a few," she responded. As soon as she was outside, she sucked in the fresh cool air. Tucker's idea about having his wines in The Painted Duck had rocked her. There were no other restaurants of that caliber in town. She could try the same tactic in Traverse City or maybe Ludington, but she had hoped for hometown support.

Gabe watched as Charity walked out by herself. He was pleased with that, but when he was settling his bar tab, he saw Tucker leave, also. He quickly went to the back lot and got in his car. He pulled out onto the street in time to see them pass by. The two sports cars were easy to follow with their bright colors flashing under the streetlights. His dark green car blended in with the traffic. He was quite upset when he saw that they were going to the pier. It was a place where lovers walked in the evening. He felt a sharp pain in his gut.

He parked his car far away from a parking lot light and kept his eyes peeled on the figures as they moved away from him. The lighthouse was backlit with the setting sun, its tall white spire capped with a black parapet which housed the light. It was a perfect shot for even an amateur photographer. He could see Tucker take her hand; then they stopped to kiss. She pulled back quickly, he was sure of it. Didn't she? She didn't look angry, just maybe a little stand-offish. She had not leaned in for more or gazed into his eyes. Her body language did not suggest that the kiss would be leading to more. That was good. Very good. When he saw that they were coming back to their cars, he left. He didn't want to be around to see the goodnight kiss.

Chapter Eight

Covers twisted around her legs, the pillow was too hard, the sheets too hot. There was no slumber to be found in her bed that night. Charity's mind wouldn't stop working as she went over and over what had occurred between her and Tucker. She had needed to sort it all out before sleep would come. She wanted to make sure she was not a girl of loose morals, going from one man to the next. After replaying every word and nuance of the dinner last night, she was sure there was nothing, and there would be nothing, between the two of them. The kiss was nice, but that was it. Just nice. Not like with --. 'No! Stop!' she told herself. She had felt no fireworks, at all; there was no host of angels singing, and she was sure Tucker hadn't heard any, either.

With her lack of sleep, it had been difficult to get moving in the morning, and she had to be in the office on time. Her father was watching her every move. She was looking forward to calling contractors, so she could get her facts in order before presenting her plans to her dad. When she came down for breakfast, she discovered an empty kitchen; he had already left and her mother was nowhere around. That was good. She didn't want to face her dad when she was in such a rush. She was sure he would find something to criticize. He had always been a good dad, but she was beginning to see that he was a very strict boss. She grabbed a dry piece of toast that had been left out on the counter, found her car keys in the dish by the door, and hurried out, but as soon as she rounded the car to get to the driver's side, she noticed two flat tires.

"Now, how did that happen?" she said aloud. Everything had been perfectly fine when she came home last night. Maybe she had picked up some nails in the driveway, causing a slow leak – but on the same side of the car? "Shoot. Now what?" Charity ran back in to change her shoes. She quickly put on her running shoes, and took a tote bag out of the closet for her heels. She began to walk the short distance to the pole barn that held the offices. It wasn't that far, but she needed to get to the barn later, and that was a good hike away; she had planned to drive her car from the office. As soon as she entered the office building, she went to her father's door. He was leaning back in his chair, reading a winemaker's journal.

"Sorry, I'm late, Dad. I've got two flat tires on my car."

"Two? Now that's odd. You probably picked up some debris in the driveway. Did you change it?" Then he laughed when he saw the look on her face. He knew there was no way in the world his baby girl was going to change a flat tire. "I'll get one of the men to take care of it for you. Do you need it right away? Most of them are already in the fields."

"I have some phone calls to make, and then I'm heading out to the old barn. But it's a nice day for a walk. No problem. Thanks, Dad."

Charity got right to work once she was in her office space. She called several contractors for estimates on the septic tank, and then she contacted a few builders in the area that she knew about the restroom facilities. One was in the neighborhood on a building project and said he could meet her at the barn in an hour. That gave her time to line up her questions, so she didn't sound too ignorant. She was totally engrossed in her thoughts and charts when her phone rang.

"Hello, Diamante Wines. Charity Henley here."

"Hi, Char, it's Tucker."

"Good morning, Tucker. And by the way, I don't like being called Char. You can hear what happened when you preceded it with hi. It became highchair. I had enough teasing with that in elementary school."

"Oh, sorry," he laughed. "I hadn't thought of it that way. Nothing like getting started on the wrong foot."

"No problem, really. Just for future reference, Charity is fine." Charity suddenly felt on edge. She wondered why she felt so irritated. Maybe the lack of sleep was getting to her combined with the flats. "What can I do for you?"

"I just called to say that I enjoyed our evening, and wondered if we could do it again sometime." His voice sounded sweet and anxious, but as Charity remembered from last night, he seemed just as eager to end their date after their walk as she had been. She wondered why he would be pursuing her, when things did not go as smoothly as they could have. He was Tucker Morrison, for Pete's sake. He could ask anyone out he wanted. Was there such a shortage of women in this town?

"Well, actually, Tucker. I have a lot of work to do. I'm so far out of the loop as to what goes on in this business, that I'll need all of my extra time to study up on growing grapes and making wine."

"I can help with that, and I'd love nothing more than coaching you," he suggested, his tone as smooth as butter.

"Uh, thanks, Tuck, but I really need to do this on my own. My job depends on proving to my Dad that I'm a grown-up now and can handle new challenges." He didn't seem to be backing down from her gentle rebuff.

"I understand. Of course. But if you need anything in the future, please don't hesitate to call. I'll help in any way I can."

"Thanks for understanding, Tucker. I'll settle down soon and then maybe we can catch lunch. How's that?"

"Sure, fine, I'll look forward to your call. Talk to you later." He had ended the call quite curtly. She was sure he was upset with her.

Charity wondered what had possessed her to bring up going to lunch with him. She had already established a way out, and now, because she was too weak to turn him away completely, she had left the door open again. That had always been her problem; she couldn't say no. She felt the heat rise up on her neck and then the flush to her cheeks. Charity busied herself with minor tasks to erase any thoughts that had surfaced, then she grabbed a light jacket and began the walk to the barn.

An access drive cut across the grapevine fields allowing the workers to get to a specific area by car or truck that needed attention for pruning or picking. At the end of the dirt drive, on the far side of the Henley property, is where the barn stood, so tall and huge that it was visible from the main house, even though it was many acres away. It was actually close to the Morrison property line. The first row of Sonny Rosso Vineyard grapes were planted a quarter of a mile away from the barn in order to prevent diseases that were air born from hopping over. This dead zone had been a sore spot between the two land owners. Dan Morrison wanted to use every inch of his land for growing grapes, but he blamed Spencer Henley for planting too close to the line, although Spencer had planted there first, before Dan had expanded the original Rosso field. Morrison's idea was that Spencer should give up another acre of planting, and he would leave one fallow acre on his side of the line and that would leave the space Morrison felt was needed to separate the farms. Spencer refused to move his grapes. They were established and had been there for years before Morrison had begun to plant in the area. It took grapes a minimum of three years before they produced enough to sell or use in their own winery. It just so happened this variety had been his best producer. Even though their difference of opinion had begun with casual conversation, it had later turned to many heated arguments, and now there was a total breakdown of communication. The men no longer talked to each other, and preferred not to hear the other's name mentioned in their presence.

Charity's walk to the barn was quite pleasant; it was a beautiful day, and she really appreciated the chance to stretch her legs. She noticed the tiny little green balls already forming on the vines. By harvest time they would be large and juicy and would have turned all shades of purple or red, depending on the variety. The large leaves looked healthy, dark green, and with no visible sign of insects, always a good thing. The rest was up to Mother Nature, a farmer's best friend or worst enemy and completely out of his control. A good season could produce an award winning bottle; a bad weather season could cause total disaster and huge financial loss. Growing grapes was a gamble, but once it was in the blood of the farmer, most found it difficult to let go.

As Charity approached the barn, she saw a pickup truck parked in front of the door and a man walking around with a clipboard in hand. Her contractor had already arrived. "Hi," she called out.

"Hey." He began to walk toward her as soon as he called out his greeting. He was about forty-five or fifty, wore the typical jeans and plaid shirt, and had a straw cowboy hat on his head. As he neared, he extended his hand, saying, "I'm Jim Holtz, and you must be Miss Henley."

"Yes, I am. Nice to meet you. Sorry you had to wait. I walked over from the office building, and it took a little longer than I thought."

"No problem," said Jim. "It gave me a chance to walk around the exterior and look over the structure. I took some measurements and made an assessment based on the layout of the land and the nearness of the well. Hope you don't mind."

"Of course not. I'm glad you got started. Let me unlock the door so you can get a look at the interior."

Once inside, Jim began measuring, using both an old-fashioned tape measure and his laser device. He studied beams and posts for structural damage, strength, rot, and safety, making notes and calculations on his tablet. "Man, this barn is amazing. It always surprises me how well they hold up if they are taken care of along the way. Where were you thinking the restrooms might go?"

"Over here in the tack room area." She pointed toward the small room she had been in with Gabe to warm by the fire. She wasn't sure what she had been thinking that day, the way she had responded to him was embarrassing. She choked back a sob and tried to clear her head.

"Are you okay?" asked the contractor.

"Yes, sorry, I guess I had some dust in my throat. So what do you think? Is it feasible?"

"Sure, I can make it work. It's on the side of the barn closest to the well so that helps. We'll have to have a septic tank dug, but it could be in the area along the property line close to this unplanted area of the Morrison property. That way it won't interfere with the grapevines. Of course, that has to be cleared with the County. But I've seen it done before. I don't expect a problem."

"Good, and I thought we could have a small kitchenette along this wall at the back of the tack room so it would be close to the water pipes. Just a sink and some counter space with a few cupboards above. That would be helpful for any caterers a party might use. Oh, and we also need a small bar with a wall rack for the wines. I suppose that should have running water, too. Maybe over here?"

"Sure I can do that. How about a wine cooler and a refrigerator/freezer for ice?"

"Oh, I almost forgot about that. Yes, we will definitely need a fridge."

Jim stood in the middle of the barn and slowly turned around as he looked up and down. "I see the stairs to the loft look in good shape. Mind if I take a look up there?"

"Go ahead. I'll follow you up." Charity's legs began to tremble. This was probably the first time anyone other than her or Gabe had been in the loft in years. She had not been up here in over two years, herself.

When they got to the opening, Jim stood on the loft flooring and laughed. "Looks like someone's been camping out."

"Oh, that's just my old playroom."

"Really?" he questioned, with a twinkle in his eye. "We all had a playroom like that around these parts. I remember mine well." He chuckled, but when he saw her embarrassment, he changed the subject quickly. She was a client after all, and he realized he should not have been so impertinent. "I'm sorry, miss. That was out of line."

"No problem. It's not what you think." 'Although it is, isn't it,' she thought. 'Or was. No, no more. Never again.'

"I don't see any problems up here, at all. We might have to enclose the steps, though, so your clients or their kids don't come up here. It could be a major liability. If someone fell off the loft, you could be sued, big time."

"Yes, we'd better work that into the plans, as well. I hadn't thought of that."

"Let's go back down. I can do a rough sketch of my idea, but later I'll send over an actual rendering, with costs, so you can make your decision."

"Sounds good, Jim. I'd like to present this to my father as soon as possible. If I get the go-ahead, how soon can this project be completed? I'd like to have it ready before the fall harvest."

"I think we can manage that. It should only take a couple of months, if we don't run into unexpected problems, and of course, if the weather cooperates when the septic tank needs to be dug."

"Okay, then. Thanks Jim. The sooner you can get me the estimates, the sooner I can talk to my dad about the whole thing."

"I'll have it to you by the end of the week, or before. It was nice working with you, Miss Henley."

"Just Charity, please. Thanks for coming out, Jim."

Chapter Nine

She listened to the familiar creak of the steps as he descended the stairs. The sound of the barn door as he slid it closed reassured her that she was alone, but, still, she didn't move a muscle until she heard the pickup truck leave the property. Standing in the middle of her old sanctuary and looking at it through Jim's eyes, she could see why he had made assumptions. The bedding on the mattress was fresh and clean. A bright orange comforter was neatly placed over the turned-down yellow sheets. Floral pillow shams protected the pillows from dust, and on the crate which had always been used as a side table, someone had left a vase of yellow daffodils. 'Someone? Who am I kidding?' she thought. It was Gabe, of course. It could be no one else. There was no one around the farm who would be interested in the old barn other than herself. He knew she would eventually come to check out her old space. In anticipation of her return, he had hung bright red, Chinese paper lanterns from some of the beams, and there was an old-world tapestry nailed to the wall behind the mattress, serving as a headboard of sorts. The colors were a crazy mishmash, but it all came together beautifully. No one could possibly mistake this as a child's playroom. Now she was mortified with the assumptions that Jim must have had about her. But she consoled herself with the idea that perhaps he had thought the new decorations were done by someone else. After all, he didn't know a thing about her history here – their history.

Tears filled her eyes as she recalled her last day, here. It was two years ago, the day that Belle and Brick got married. She had made it through the ceremony and reception. Smiled through the whole thing and passed on her congratulations. She had even been able to give a toast and make light of her infatuation with Brick as a small child. But the pain she held inside almost tore her apart. Then, after all of the guests had left and Belle and Brick were well on their way to their honeymoon in Hawaii, she had excused herself, saying she needed to walk off all of the food she had consumed. And, of course, she had headed straight to her loft hideout in the barn. She knew he would be there. He was always there when she needed him. How he knew she would come, she had no idea, but they had always had a connection that seemed to traverse the cosmos. When she slid the barn door open, he was already inside, waiting for her. She went straight to his arms and sobbed. He held her for a long time, not saying a word, just letting her cry it out. Then he took her hand and led her up the stairs. She knew what was coming next, and so did he. It was what he wanted, what he always wanted when he was with her. She didn't object; in fact, she never did. Whatever happened was all on her. She could have stopped it at any moment, knowing he would have complied. But she needed him – she needed him to ease her pain.

This time there had been more passion than ever before between the two of them, much more than simple lovemaking. Charity was releasing all the pent-up emotions of the day, but for Gabe it was his chance to express his feelings. He wanted to help her through this difficult day, but at the same time he was hoping that now that Belle and Brick were finally together legally, Charity would commit to him. He needed to show her how much he cared, how desperately in love with her he truly was. He was sure this time she felt his desire and need for her. He needed to profess his love and he intended to do so, but when they were spent and lying in each other's arms, he could feel her slowly pull away, as her emotions and physical need subsided.

From Charity's viewpoint, she had just humiliated herself. Letting herself go like that with Gabe when she had felt so much for Brick was unthinkable. When she had tried to apologize to Gabe, he had been furious. He said he didn't need an apology and didn't want one. He asked her if she thought he was the kind of man who would take advantage of her pain. He said he thought she knew him better than that. He said she had wanted to make love just as much as he had; and it wasn't the first time. She had gone upstairs willingly. No one had forced her.

She accused him of using her while she was in a fragile state. She said he knew she had always been in love with Brick. *He* accused *her* of using him to replace Brick. She had always used him in that way, and he had allowed it, but no more, he said. The fight continued as they got dressed, and ended up with Charity slapping his face, saying she never wanted to see him again. And that's where they had left it. After that, he made sure he was never around whenever she came home for the summer or during the holidays. She had not seen him until that day in the barn when she had first returned home after graduation. As she stood in the loft, looking at the effort he had put into making everything just right for her, she could see that he had not given up on her. Gabe, her rock, would always be there. How could she get through to him that she did not want a man in her life in the way that he wanted to be? It was too painful when that man didn't return the love. She was going to have a career; she would take care of herself; she would make sure she would never need a man again. But she knew now that she didn't want to lose Gabe, either. How could she explain to him, without hurting him, that she needed him as a friend, but only as a friend? Charity knew she would have to do some soul searching in order to discover why she had such a weakness for Gabe, she would need to ask for God's forgiveness, and then she would have to beg Gabe to forgive her.

Mateo watched as Charity returned to her office. She walked quietly into the room without a greeting or a wave of the hand, then she closed the door behind her. Something was seriously bothering that girl. He hoped her family was aware of how troubled she was. The change in personality had begun during her last year of high school. Before that she had been a happy, outgoing girl. When she was a child she was often found singing to herself or dancing in the fields without a care in the world that anyone was watching. As she grew to become a teen, she began to be slightly more guarded, as most young girls do, but she was still sweet and loving. Mateo had always held a special place in his heart for the girl. And he could tell by looking at his son's face every time she was near what he thought of her, although not a word of it had ever been mentioned. Mateo believed that he should not press the issue. He always tried to stay out of Gabe's business unless he came to him for advice or help, which he rarely did. Gabe was the kind of man who harbored intense feelings, but he usually preferred to deal with them on his own. Mateo noticed he was happiest when he was with Charity, but lately something was off. He couldn't understand why the two young folks had not even acknowledged each other's existence since she had returned home.

Perhaps tonight would be different. He smiled to himself in anticipation.

Charity was standing at the window in her office, gazing out at nothing. She was trying to stop all of the thoughts that were rolling around in her mind. She had always perceived herself to be a 'good girl,' even though there was a time when she had let the world believe differently. She actually had a strong moral code; it had been taught to her by a deeply religious mother. Her father came off as a tolerant and generous man when it came to raising his daughter, but as far as her behavior was concerned, he was very strict. When she was young her curfew was much earlier than some of the other girls, and all sleepover parties were checked out with the other parents first. Her mother always waited up for her when she went on a date, insisting on a kiss goodnight so she could get close enough to check for alcohol. Charity would never think of disappointing them in that way; she left that kind of behavior up to Trey. And that was the reason why she couldn't get her head around her behavior when she was with Gabe. She felt as if she had let them down as well as herself. Letting go, like she had, showed a total lack of self-control. It couldn't happen again. She wouldn't allow it. She decided the best course was to steer clear of Mr. Gabriel Rivera.

The rest of Charity's day went fairly well. She busied herself compiling facts and figures for the barn renovation. That way, as soon as she got the drawing and details from Jim Holtz, she could present her plan to her father in a professional way. She wanted him to see that her education had not been wasted. She waited out the rest of the day for the plan and estimate to come through by fax or delivery, but it never arrived, so she locked up her office and headed home.

As she was walking to the house, she passed the small, rustic chapel her father had built for her mother. Her mother had requested it right after her baby had been kidnapped. In the agonizing days and nights that followed, Hope had felt a need for the quiet retreat, and she was often seen praying on her knees with her rosary in hand. The devastated mother was aware that others might have troubles of their own, and even in her misery, she took the time to make sure it was always kept open during the day for any of the farm hands who might also feel a need to talk to God. On occasion, a few special weddings had even been held here. It was a sacred place and Charity had been taught at a young age to respect the chapel. It was not a playhouse, her mother had said, when she found her sitting in the pews with her dolls one day. But the scolding had ended with a kiss as her mother explained how the chapel could be a special place to go to God to ask Him to help her with her problems or to give thanks for her blessings. Then one day, when she was seventeen, Charity had found herself there seeking solace after her first time with Gabe. She had fallen on her knees, when the enormity and shame of what she had done hit her full force. She had not taken it lightly like some teens did who were sexually active. Each time, after that, she promised herself it would be the last, but each time the pull to Gabe's arms was so powerful, that she was incapable of resisting. He was her safe haven and her comfort. 'How could that be wrong?' she asked God. But each time she had left more confused than when she had entered.

For a brief fleeting moment, Charity thought about stopping in the chapel today, but she was running late as far as dinner was concerned, and her mother preferred every member of the family to be seated at the table at the same time. Maybe tomorrow she could find time to go. It would do no good for her parents to know that she was troubled, so she put on her happy face, and went in the house.

"Hi, Mom. I'm home."

"Oh, hi, Charity. I'm glad you made it in time. We're having guests for dinner."

"Anyone special?" asked Charity.

Her parents often entertained business contacts at the dinner table. They found their home environment very conducive to making a friendly deal. Charity had grown up with strangers at the table, and perhaps that was the reason she had always gotten along with people so well. She could be a charmer when she set her mind to it. The darling little girl who often flirted with Brick had turned into a real beauty. And other than a few rebellious months when she was 16, her parents were very proud of the way she handled herself -- until she was 17, that is. At that time they noticed a drastic personality change, but they chalked it up to Belle's return and having to deal with the adjustment of a new family member. Charity's world had been completely upset, but she seemed to come around when she went off to college. What they didn't realize is that she was only covering her pain. Her displacement in the family and her loss of Brick, both at the same time, had almost put her under. Only Sid and Gabe knew the extent of her misery.

"I think you'll be thrilled with our guests tonight. I'll save who it is as a surprise. Now, go put on something nice."

"I always do, Mom," she laughed. Her mother was quite transparent at times. She was probably setting her up with a date. 'Great,' she thought, 'that's all I need.'

Charity changed into a new spring dress she had recently purchased. She had been waiting for the right time to wear it. It had a tight fighting bodice, a sweetheart neckline, a belted waist, and a flared skirt, much like the style of the 1940s. She had always enjoyed experimenting with clothes, and she especially enjoyed styles of other eras. This particular design conformed to her shape perfectly. The bright rose color gave the outfit a modern flare and complimented her warm complexion and dark hair which she had twisted up. She wore a gold charm bracelet and a simple gold chain with a cross around her neck. She added the small diamond earrings her father had given her on her 18th birthday. After a twirl in the full-length mirror, she decided she was satisfied with what she saw. Charity was not in the market for a new man in her life, if that is what her mother had planned, but she was starting to think in terms of the business, now. She might be able to make an impression in that way, on the client or whoever it was, and at the same time, please her father with her people skills.

She could hear voices as the guests arrived. The rumbling timbre told her there was more than one male. 'Oh well, here goes.' she sighed. She walked into the room just as her father was greeting Mateo and his wife, Maria, -- and their son, Gabe.

Chapter Ten

Gabe turned when he felt her enter the room. They gazed at each other for a fraction of a second, not long enough for the parents to notice that there was some tension floating across the room. Gabe had never seen her look more beautiful; his heart was aching for her, wanting to go to her, placing kisses on her beautiful neck and mouth. Charity couldn't figure out why her heart had skipped a beat; it was only Gabe, her childhood friend.

Mateo came forward, "Oh Charity, how are you? You look lovely tonight. You remember my Maria, right?"

"Of course. Mrs. Rivera, nice to see you again." As she hugged Maria hello, Charity glanced at Gabe over his mother's shoulder. She knew what was coming next.

"And of course, you know Gabe," said Mateo.

They stepped awkwardly toward each other. Charity began to extend her hand, but Gabe moved in for a hug. He quietly whispered in her ear, "You look fantastic. Am I forgiven, Tee?" He felt her quick nod next to his cheek, and when he pulled back, flashing his gorgeous smile, he noticed tears beginning to glisten in her eyes, eyes that could melt a man's soul, eyes that held a story only the two of them knew.

Even though they couldn't hear what Gabe had whispered to Charity, the two sets of parents had not missed any of the exchange. They couldn't help but see the longing look exposed on Gabe's face, and his tender touch when he had wrapped his arms around her. Charity was somewhat shaken and confused as usual whenever she was around Gabe these days, but she recovered by saying, "When do we eat, Mama? I'm starving."

That one simple sentence kick-started the laughter and conversation among the men, as the women began to carry the platters of food to the table.

Maria and Hope chattered on in Spanish, while Charity tried to keep up with the language that both women had grown up with. Sometimes they used English words interspersed with the Spanish, known as Spanglish, and that helped her to follow the content. She tried her best to speak Spanish as quickly as they did, but without using it regularly, it was impossible. They laughed and corrected her grammar every now and then, but overall, they said she did very well.

When the meal was ready, they all took their chairs at the direction of Hope. Charity's mother – 'of course,' thought Charity, -- had seated her next to Gabe. She was beginning to suspect the two women had a plan. Gabe didn't mind one bit; he was very happy with the seating arrangement. He bumped into her hand whenever he could, purposely reaching for the same thing as an excuse to touch. He yearned to do more, perhaps place a hand on her knee, but he restrained himself with their parents furtively watching their every move. He could have sworn he saw his dad wink at his mother, as she smiled at Hope, which then moved to a nod to Spencer. It could have just been part of their conversation gestures, but he thought it more likely a secret communication between them. He wondered if they were rooting for him or if he had misinterpreted their body language. If they were, it gave him more resolve to pursue Charity and make her realize that she belonged to him. His heart was full of joy; his parents and hers were hoping for a union between the families. He could see that now. He had never been sure of how the Henleys felt about him, other than being their employee's kid, and now their mechanic and field manager. He had always held them in high regard, but he felt the difference because their financial status was at a much higher level than that of his family. But, in fact, Gabe had always misread their friendship. The Henleys considered the Riveras to be among their best friends. They had acknowledged long ago that they could not have kept this vineyard going without Mateo. He was the recipient of healthy bonuses every year, some of which had been placed in trust for Gabe, as well as free housing as part of his compensation package.

Gabe and Charity chatted about the past few years, and tried to keep things light and simple. Charity had not felt so relaxed in quite a while. Conversation with Gabe was always easy. Maybe it was the wine, or being around a table with people she loved, but she had never been happier. Then, suddenly, the last thought she had spoken in her mind was replayed with a clarity she had not felt before. People she loved. She loved? People? -- or Gabe? Her heart began to pound, she felt faint, couldn't get her breath. Couldn't breathe. Needed air. Now! She pushed back her chair and bolted from the room. She ran out the front door to the porch and gasped for air.

"Gabe, what did you say to her?" chastened his mother.

"Not a thing. We were just talking. I'll find out what's wrong." He began to stand up, but Hope interceded.

No," she said. "I think she's having a panic attack. She's had them before. I'll go to her. Continue on with your meal. We'll be back soon."

She grabbed a brown paper bag that she kept within easy reach in the cupboard. She found Charity sitting on the swing, doubled over, -- desperately trying to suck in some air. She placed the bag over her mouth and said gently, "Breathe slowly, baby girl."

In a matter of minutes, Charity was breathing normally. She fell into her mother's arms and sobbed. "Oh, mama, I'm such a mess."

"I doubt that very much, mija." She patted her and comforted her for a few moments, then said, "Are you okay now? Let's go around the house to the back door, so you can go in the bathroom without being seen. Wash your face with cool water, and I'll explain to the rest of them. They are so concerned for you. Then we'll go on with our meal. We can talk about the mess in your life tomorrow; all right, my sweet?"

"Okay, mama. Thank you."

Hope went back to the table when she was sure Charity was going to be okay. She explained that Charity had had these attacks since she was a teen, and they came on unexpectedly. She was fine now, she said; she would return soon.

When Charity came into the room, Gabe stood up so quickly that he almost overturned his chair. "Are you okay?" he asked.

"I'm fine, Gabe. Can we just forget it?" He nodded to her weakly and helped her to her chair as if she were an invalid. The gesture did not go unnoticed by the rest of the group.

The meal and following drinks moved along normally with the help of the conversing parents. Charity was pretty quiet, but she held it together until they were saying their goodbyes. Gabe leaned in, gave her a hug that was quite a bit more familiar than the first time, and whispered, "I'll call you tomorrow."

Charity said quietly, "Okay," but he noticed, that for a few seconds she stared deeply into his eyes as if looking for something. It was exactly what he needed to give him hope once again.

They all stepped outside for the final goodbyes, except for Charity who excused herself and retreated to her room. She lay down on her bed, not even taking the time to remove her shoes. 'What happened tonight?' she wondered. Everything was fine until she started to think about – love. 'No,' she screamed in her head.

"I will not fall in love," she said out loud, startled by her own anger. She punched her fist into her pillow. "Never again!"

Voices were heard outside her bedroom window which was directly above the porch. They seemed to be trying to start a car that was refusing to turn over. Charity turned off the lights in her room, so she could look out without being detected. It looked like Gabe's car was the only one out there. He must have come with his parents in the same vehicle.

"I don't understand this. It was fine when we arrived. Doesn't make sense."

"I'll bring my car around and give you a lift home. We can figure it out tomorrow when it's light out," said Spencer.

"Don't bother," said Mateo, "we can walk."

"I wouldn't think of letting you walk across the field in the dark. I'll just be a minute." A few minutes later, Charity heard them all get in the car and drive away. It wasn't long before her father returned, but by then she had already drifted into a restless sleep.

Charity woke from her slumber with tears streaking down her face and frown lines on her forehead. Images of Brick had flashed through her dreams, but oddly, they were not the same romantic visions she had had for years. She saw Brick as a husband to her sister and a father to their new baby. He tossed a baby high as they both laughed; she had never seen him look happier. One part of the dream consisted of her and Belle on the porch swing as Belle told her how much she loved her and that she was so thankful for being connected to the family again. Next, Charity turned from Belle to look back at Brick, but he began to fade away. She screamed for him to come back, but it was no use. She stretched out her arms to him, but he was getting farther and farther from her reach. Then suddenly she saw him walking down the lane with Belle. His arm was around her as she leaned her head on his shoulder. She carried a sweet baby in her arms. Charity felt an arm around her also, and turned to look into Gabe's compassionate eyes. He tried to pull her in to comfort her, but she rejected him, and pushed him away. He looked so hurt, but she couldn't help it. She never wanted to love another man in her life. She was crying hysterically in her dream, and woke up with tears still wet on her eyelids. Charity sat up abruptly in bed and wondered why she had been so upset. She was resolved to the fact that Belle and Brick were together now, and she was following through with her plan to live life the way she wanted, without a man. She would be fine on her own. She didn't need anyone. She didn't want anyone.

The sound of a tow truck rattling down the drive and voices explaining the problem with Gabe's car, jarred her enough to look at the clock. She had to get moving. She glanced out the window to see Gabe's vehicle being towed away. Strange -- Gabe was a top-notch mechanic, why would he need professional help?

At the breakfast table, she casually asked her mother what was wrong with Gabe's car.

"He thinks someone put sugar in the gas tank," replied Hope.

"Sugar? Who would do that? And in front of the house while we were having a meal? That's unbelievable!"

"Yes, it is, and a little frightening that someone who wants to do damage would come so close to us."

Hope placed a lightly-browned waffle on Charity's plate. "Syrup?" she asked.

Charity nodded, already buttering her warm and delicious morning meal. "I guess they knew that we were busy, and it was dark enough out so they couldn't be seen."

"I'm upset with myself for not leaving the porch light on. But when the Riveras arrived, the sun hadn't set yet, and I never thought of it until they were leaving."

"I can't imagine who would want to cause trouble. It seems like a very vindictive thing to do."

"And costly," said her mother. "Now about last night. You want to talk about it?"

"Not today, Mama. I'm running late as usual. I'll be okay. I just need to work out a few things. Don't worry."

"I'm a mother," she smiled. "I always worry."

Charity excused herself leaving half of her waffle behind, gave a quick kiss to her mother, and then walked the short distance to the winery. The first thing she saw when she entered her office was a fax sheet waiting for her. She smiled, excited to present the proposal to her Dad. He would love the plan -- she knew it. She gave it a quick look, nodding with approval. It was exactly what she had expected and more. She gathered up her papers, and headed to her father's office.

"Morning, Dad."

"Morning, baby girl. You look perky today."

"I have something exciting to talk to you about. Do you have time?

"Sure, just let me finish inputting this figure, before I lose what I was doing."

Charity roamed around his office, looking at all of the gold medals and framed certificates hanging on his wall. She had seen them many times before, but now she was looking at them as an adult with her own personal stake in the wine business. Her father was so proud that they had been chosen to receive so many awards for their great wines. Each August the Michigan Wine Competition was held in Lansing.

Over half of the 115 wineries in Michigan were present on any given year, depending on the harshness of the previous winter and the rainfall of the summer months. Weather was a big factor in the production and taste. And a bad year could turn the grapes used for a great wine into a mediocre wine, which of course would not be entered that year. So far her father had always been able to stay ahead of the problems that could occur, but it was a shaky business and not for the faint of heart.

"Okay, what can I do for you?" he said as he closed his laptop.

"Well," said Charity clearing her throat in order to make a clear and concise presentation, "I have some facts and figures worked up for my proposal."

Spencer smiled, so proud at how well she had matured. He sat back to give her his full attention. "Go ahead."

Charity went on to explain her idea with the barn, and then she showed him the estimate for construction and the needed septic tank. "Not bad," he said. "Did you figure in the permit fee and inspections?"

"Yes, Mr. Holtz has worked all of that in. You can see it listed here." She leaned over to point to a column of numbers. "It's the new trend, Dad, getting married in barns. You have to admit our setting is beautiful and the barn is unique in that it's still standing and solid at that. The extra income from renting out the venue and the sale of wine will be a boost, as well as help to promote our brand. And once we're established, I thought we could offer adult hayrides in the fall leaving from the barn and circling through the vineyard and back for a nice warm mulled wine."

"I have thought about that over the years, but we don't have any horses."

"It can be done with a tractor. Maybe down the road we can buy an antique hit-and-miss John Deere, or an antique Allis-Chalmers, just to add to the ambiance."

"Hmm, that would give me a good excuse to buy an old tractor. I've always wanted to own a hit-and-miss engine, but I could never convince Mother there was a need for one. But let's take it slow. First things first. I think you've got a good idea, here. And the price seems fair. I like Jim. I'm sure he'll do a great job. What's his timeline?"

"He says if he gets started now, he can have it finished in time for fall harvest. We can start to advertise and take reservations before he's finished. And I can move ahead with the decorating plans at the same time."

"Who will take care of the bookings, deposits, setup, and cleanup, etc.?" asked Spencer.

"I'll do it at first, and if we get too busy, then I'll have to hire a manager."

"Sounds like you've thought of everything." He paused a moment to let her squirm a little. "Okay, I'll give you my go ahead, but I want to see progress reports regularly."

"Thanks, Dad. I think you're going to be happy with it."

"Anything else?" he asked. "Got any more ideas that will tap into my checkbook?" He chuckled. He had always had a hard time denying her anything.

Charity smiled and gave him a hug. "I do have other ideas, but they can wait. One has already been foiled, I guess. I'll fill you in later. But for now, I'd better go call Jim. I want him to get started as soon as possible. We can't really advertise until we have a good start on the renovation." And with that she was off to make the call, and begin the project that would prove to her father that she can handle being a career woman in an adult world.

Chapter Eleven

Tucker sat in his car outside of the Diamante Vineyard offices. He knew that Charity had said she would call when she was ready to see him again, but he couldn't wait any longer. He needed to see her now, it was important in order for his plans to go forward. He picked up the tube of rolled up papers on the seat next to him, looked in the mirror, and smoothed and fluffed his hair with his fingers. He was quite nervous; this meant so much to him.

On the way toward her office door, he made a last minute decision and took a detour to her father's office instead. He tapped lightly, and was immediately called in.

"Good morning, Mr. Spencer. How are you?" said Tucker, with a smile and as much respect as he could muster.

"Oh, hello, Tucker. Come in. What brings you here this morning?" Spencer was more than a little puzzled as to why Tucker Morrison was in his office, since the families were not on the best of terms.

"I wanted to talk to you about something, if you don't mind. Do you have a minute? Did I interrupt anything?"

"I was just going over the schedule for the wine competition in the fall, but that can wait. You've got me curious. Have a seat."

Tucker was nervous, but he hoped it didn't show. A lot was riding on this conversation. He cleared his throat and proceeded. "I'm not sure if you're aware, but I've run into Charity a few times since she's been back. You know, we dated for a short while in high school."

"Yes, I remember." Spencer was getting impatient now.

"Well, actually, I ran into her once at The Painted Duck, and I asked her out on a date, which we also had a few days later at The Duck."

Spencer stiffened slightly. "No, I wasn't aware of that."

Tucker looked for an expression or gesture which would alert him to Spencer's feelings about what had been said, but he saw nothing that was meant to deter him, so he forged ahead.

"We have a lot in common with the grape growing and wine producing, plus we know a lot of the same people. I'd really like to see her again. I know that we're both adults, but it would mean a lot to me if you would give your approval, since there's bad history between our families." Tucker tried to read Spencer's face, but figured he must be a great poker player, because he could detect nothing on his stone-blank expression. He decided it was time to stop talking now and wait for Charity's father to speak.

There was an awkward pause for a moment, then Spencer said without a smile, "Yes, your father and I have had problems that he doesn't seem to want to mend, even though I've made many attempts, but I won't hold that against you. So if Charity wants to go out with you, that's her business, but just beware that I'll be watching. She's still my little girl, and I won't allow you or anyone else to hurt her."

"Yes, sir, I understand. I would never hurt her, you can be sure. Thank you. And rest assured, I am not my father; I operate with a different code altogether." As Tucker stood to go, he noticed that even though the big man in the chair had spoken words of acceptance, his face didn't show it, so Tucker said his goodbyes and removed himself from the room as quickly as possible.

Outside the door, Tucker was visibly shaken; he was surprised at how afraid of Spencer Henley he had been. So much was riding on Mr. Henley's answer, but now he had his approval to go ahead. So the next stop was Charity's office. He had to play it smoothly, or he could be rejected here, as well.

Charity looked up at the first sound of the knock. It could only be her father. She hadn't established herself enough yet to have visitors. "Enter," she said in a silly, royal-like way she would have only used on her dad. She was surprised to see Tucker at her door.

"Oh, Tuck, I thought I was going to call *you*, and now here you are in my office again." When she saw the look on Tucker's face, she realized immediately how harsh she sounded, and tried to tone it down with a laugh.

"Sorry, Char – I mean, Charity. I have something I wanted to talk to you about. Can you give me a few minutes?"

"Sure. I'm not that busy yet." She laughed at the thought that anyone would think her day was so peppered with appointments that they could interrupt anything. "What's on your mind?" She hoped it wasn't another date. She wasn't sure she was ready for anything like that yet, especially after her latest panic attack.

"Well, I got this project going with The Painted Duck, or I was hoping it would be a project, but I'm still not sure. I was wondering if you could help me."

This was definitely something she didn't want to hear. The Painted Duck had been one of her dreams. Having their wine label there exclusively was part of her plan, and she had had to make drastic changes in her mindset when Tucker told her he had planned to buy it. She knew that if he bought the grill, her wines would never be allowed on the premises. But at this point she didn't want him to know what she had been thinking.

"How can I help?"

"I have some plans drawn up for the changes I want to make, and I'd like to present them to my father for approval before we make our bid, but it's out of my wheelhouse. Could you take a look at them?"

He had no idea what he was asking. She had her own project with plans that she had just presented to her own father, and she was capable of helping Tucker, but did she want to? She thought for just a split second. It appeared to her that her chances of getting access to The Duck was out. Tucker's father was a force to be reckoned with. If he decided he wanted The Duck for Tucker, he would get it. The only man ever to stand up to Dan Morrison and win was her father.

"Okay, I'll take a look. But it could be a conflict of interest, so just this one time. I can't continue to help." Charity knew her father would not approve, but she had a good heart, and always found it hard to say no to anyone.

"I understand. Thank you." He began to unroll his plans, which showed removal of walls, moving the bar, and eliminating the sports bar side completely.

"I'm, uh, I'm surprised. This is drastic. Very pretty but drastic. Will the regulars continue to come without the sports bar being available?"

"Well, I'm not concerned about the locals. I want to make this an upscale restaurant for the tourists. I'd like to turn the whole steakhouse side into an urban-looking, gourmet hot spot."

"It's beautiful, Tucker. But what about the off season? Will you get enough traffic? People in snowmobile outfits won't come. They'll feel too uncomfortable."

"And they won't be allowed. It's to be jacket and tie only."

"Ooh, I don't know, that's rather grand for our small town." Charity could tell by the look on his face that he was shocked that she didn't agree with his idea.

"I thought you would be on my side on this. I was hoping you could give me a convincing argument to present to my dad." He began to roll up his papers. She could see how hurt, and maybe even angry, he was.

"Just say what you feel. If it's the right way to go, I'm sure your dad will agree. Why is his permission needed? Can't you buy it on your own?"

"No, the price is too high, and I don't have any credit for such a business venture yet. I need his backing. Don't worry, I won't give up. I have something I can bargain with. He'll cave eventually."

"See? There's the Tucker spirit I remember." 'Why am I cheering him on?' she wondered.

He seemed to soften. "Thanks, Charity. I knew you would be honest. Can we continue this conversation over dinner? I'd like to collect on that next date, now." When he smiled he was oh so charming.

"Sure, Tucker. The Duck again?"

"Where else? Seven? Tonight?"

She nodded. "Let's do the bar side this time and keep it a little less formal."

He agreed, saying he wanted to watch the customer traffic through new eyes. Maybe she had been right, and he would have to change his renovation plans.

Tucker happily left the building. He had accomplished everything he had intended to get done today. He had made peace with Spencer Henley, and he had another date with Charity. It was a good feeling. Next, he needed to report to his father.

At seven, Charity was in her car, heading to The Painted Duck. Tucker had asked to pick her up at the house, but she didn't think her father would approve of her dating him, and she wasn't aware of the earlier conversation between the two men, so in order to avoid any words of conflict, she asked to meet him there. He seemed disappointed. She could tell he had wanted to walk in the bar with her on his arm. He had always had a rather large ego, and she was beginning to see that nothing much had changed. Charity had been surprised at Tucker's attention when she first returned to Frankfort, and maybe a little flattered. He was still a bit of a hometown hero; they did love their football in these parts. And anyone who could make it to play on a big ten college team and then get drafted to a pro team, would be respected for the rest of his life, here, even if nothing more ever came of it. But that had never held much weight for Charity. She was more interested in – well, she wasn't sure. Maybe, Charity thought on the drive in, loyalty, dependability, kindness, and courage were some of her prerequisites, and of course good looks, she smiled to herself. Then she realized what she was doing. A frown crossed her forehead. No! She would not plan a life with a man. You could not count on them – only her father, her brother, and Gabe had always – tears blurred her eyes. Why did Gabe keep coming to mind for every little thing? She slammed on the brakes which threw her body forward. She had almost run a stop sign. Charity swiped at the tears that had escaped, then continuing on, turned into the parking lot in the back for The Duck.

Tucker was already there; he had been nervously watching for her. He was seated in a booth along the front windows and had seen her car turn into the lot, so as soon as he saw her walk in, he motioned her over. Tucker got up and took her elbow, leading her to sit on the side facing the door, while he was opposite her.

"Hello, Tucker. Am I late?"

"No, not at all."

Gabe sat up straight as soon as he recognized her voice. He was in his usual booth, but because he had met some friends earlier who had just recently left, he had ended up with his back to the door, and had not yet adjusted his seating. The booths were higher than a man's head, meant to cut back noise and give a person some privacy in their conversation. But it also blocked out vision, if you were not close to the aisle. With the way Gabe was sitting, he hadn't seen either one of them come in, and with the barrier as high as it was, they had not seen him sitting with his back to their booth. Tucker had placed Charity with her back to Gabe's, so if he listened closely he could hear everything she said and some of what Tucker said. The TV was blaring loudly and there was not even a game on, so when Gabe's waitress returned to fill his glass of beer, he quietly asked if she could turned it down or at least put it on 'captions only'. She agreed with a sexy smile, and purred, "Anything for you, Gabe." Soon he could hear every word they were saying. It wasn't in his nature to follow Charity around and listen in on her conversations, but he just didn't trust Tucker. They had had regular run-ins since way back in grammar school.

After the usual exchange of pleasantries about the weather, Charity asked Tucker, "So, how did it go with your dad? Did you approach him with your plans?"

"No, not yet. I have some details to take care of first. I need to gather up some leverage, because I don't intend on being turned down."

Charity raised an eyebrow. "What kind of leverage?"

"Just some father-son stuff. He'll understand when it happens."

"Oh, so you're being cagey," she teased.

The waitress came to take their orders of burgers and fries, interrupting them for a moment, but not before Charity saw Tucker's eyes flash at her comment. 'What's with him?' she wondered.

When the waitress was gone, Tucker seemed to soften quite a bit. He leaned across the table, reaching for Charity's hand. "You look beautiful tonight. Did you notice the way the men looked at you when you walked in? Seriously, you are one of the most beautiful girls I have ever seen, certainly in this county. I'm so glad you agreed to go out with me tonight."

Charity pulled her hand back to reach for her glass of water, pretending not to notice his gesture. She didn't want to encourage his advances. Since the day she had first seen him here at The Duck, she had had a feeling that something was off. She just wanted to get through this date and go home. "Well, as you recall, it was supposed to be lunch. I'm not sure how we got to date night, Tuck." She saw his frown and proceeded immediately in order to soften the retort. "I'm very glad to see you again, but I want to make it clear that I am not in the market for a man in my life. I'm happy to see you as friends, but that's it. I've got too many other things on my mind right now. I hope you understand."

"Oh, Char,--"

"Charity," she interjected.

"Yes, Charity, sorry. You know I've always had a thing for you."

"Really? What about Mary Beth and Anna and Heidi and, oh yeah, and then there was Andrea. She thought you two were going to get married as soon as high school was over. I can only guess at how many girls you were with in college. Tucker, you were always a player, and I was just one of many on your list of toys." She saw anger flash in his eyes. "I'm teasing, Tuck. You were a good catch, and in your defense, a lot of those girls threw themselves at you."

His chest puffed up a bit at the flattery. "Sure, what red-blooded guy would have turned down what was offered – but you, Charity, you never put out. I couldn't get anywhere with you, beyond a kiss here and there. Why?"

"I liked you Tucker, but I didn't want to be another notch on your belt. I wouldn't allow myself to be used like that by any man." 'Not necessarily true,' she thought to herself. Tucker saw her blush and thought she was embarrassed about where the conversation had been heading.

"Let's talk about something else. But, keep in mind, I am more attracted to you as the days go by, and I intend to get what I never had before. You'll come around. They all do." He smiled a cocky smile.

Charity stiffened but made sure Tucker didn't see. This was a new Tucker she hadn't seen before. She smiled politely, and prayed for this meal to be over.

When Gabe heard that last comment, he almost came out of his seat. 'The guy sure has a lot of brass. Some things never change,' he fumed.

Throughout the rest of the meal, the conversation was about changes and plans for The Painted Duck. They discussed décor, layout, and menu. Gabe picked up on the fact that Tucker wanted to make a bid. He had heard that Duane was going to retire. Gabe hated to think of the changes Tucker Morrison might have in mind to what was a local institution. "Jerk," he muttered under his breath. He really wanted to leave, but he was stuck here now until they left. This clandestine stuff was not in his DNA. He was a straight out guy. Normally, if he didn't like you, he would let you know. And he sure didn't have any soft feelings for Tucker, -- that much he knew for certain.

Chapter Twelve

Tucker followed Charity out the back door of The Painted Duck in order to walk her to her car. They were both surprised at the dense fog that had rolled in. It was heavy and damp and made it difficult to find their cars in the lot. He held her elbow in a proprietary way that she was not comfortable with, but tolerated. She just wanted her 'date' to be over with and longed for her soft bed to curl up in. Charity had not realized how on edge she had been all night. Something was off with Tucker, but she couldn't put her finger on it.

"I really don't think you should drive home tonight, Charity."

"I'll be okay. I was born and raised in northern Michigan just like you. Fog is inevitable."

"I know, but this fog is different. It's very dense. I don't think you'll be able to see two feet in front of the car. I'd like you to stay at my apartment for the night, just to be safe. I'm sure it'll clear up in the morning." He leaned in and tried to stroke her cheek; she could tell a kiss was coming next, so she gently deflected while looking for her car keys.

"Thanks Tucker. I know you mean well, but I'm not ready to stay overnight with anyone. I do think you're probably right about the roads, though. So I think I'll just stay at my parents' townhouse."

"I understand." He looked a little hurt, but went on to say, "I'll follow you over to make sure you get there okay."

"Tuck, it's only a few blocks. I'll be fine."

"I insist. What kind of a gentleman would I be if I let a lady drive off in the fog all alone?" He made an exaggerated bow, much like a gentleman of high society in days of old would have done when asking a lady for a dance.

187

It made Charity laugh, so she agreed to let him follow her to the townhouse. The condo was on the beach at Lake Michigan and had been owned by her family for years. Her parents had first purchased it for clients who often came from out of town to use and enjoy. The gesture often cemented a relationship leading to contracts of large purchases of Diamante wines, but Charity and Trey had also enjoyed the use of it during their teen years. They loved to stay at the beach during the summers with friends, in order to get that all important tan and to meet new people. Trey had used it for his many girlfriends when he got older, without telling his parents, of course. They each had their own key, and as long as they left it neat and clean, no one was the wiser. Charity had offered it to Belle, her new friend, before anyone knew that she was Charity's sister, and the Henleys' long lost daughter. The morning after Belle and Brick had spent their first night there together was on another foggy night, and when they returned in the morning, Charity could tell they were falling in love. It was the first peg in destroying her dreams of being with Brick, and she had not stepped foot in the condo since. But she agreed with Tucker, the ride home was going to be treacherous. She would call her parents and tell them where she was. She was sure her mother would be relieved to know she was safe.

Gabe saw the couple walk out the back entrance and even though his car was parked in the front, he followed quietly behind. He had no idea what he was looking for; Charity had rebuffed him several times now, but he still felt very protective of her, and he didn't trust Tucker one bit. He was also surprised at the density of the fog. He watched as they walked to Charity's car, noticing how they seemed to disappear, as the mist swirled to enclose around them, hiding them from his view. He walked back through the restaurant to the front door and out to his car. He planned to follow Charity home to make sure she made it okay. He waited for her car to pass by letting a few other cars go between them. Tucker's car was right behind hers. Gabe was quite surprised when she turned off the main street to the left toward the beach parking lot. Tucker's car headed in the same direction. He knew immediately she planned to stay at her condo, but he was not happy to see that Tucker's car was going there, too.

As before, he parked a little distance away from them, but this time he was unable to see what was going on. Was she inviting Tucker in? Gabe could feel the rage as his blood began to boil at the thought of them alone together in the townhouse. He quietly got out of his car, and worked his way toward them by moving behind other cars in the lot, until he was finally close enough to hear conversation.

"Thanks, Tucker, I'll be fine now. I appreciate it."

"Of course, I wouldn't have it any other way. But I really don't want the evening to end here. I'd like to spend more time with you. I'm not ready to say goodnight. I can't let you go yet. How about a nightcap to let me wait out the fog a little?" He stroked her arm hoping to stir some feelings.

"I'm not up for a night cap. I really want to go to bed. I'm quite tired tonight for some reason. And you only have a few blocks to go to your place. I'm sure you can handle it. You made it this far, didn't you?" She smiled, trying to keep things on a friendly footing. Charity suddenly felt very uncomfortable being outside her door, alone with Tucker in the fog that had encased them like a blanket. She turned and began to fumble with the key, not able to see the keyhole easily. Tucker moved from behind, his face was very close to hers; he was cheek to cheek to her now. She could feel his breath on her neck.

"Here, let me help you," he said in a deep, raspy voice. He took the key from her hand and then pushed his body in closer to open the door. When she turned and looked up to take the key back, his mouth was on hers. He had a lot of strength, and she was unable to push him away. He was holding her arms down tightly and pushing her back in towards the open door. He stopped a moment, pinned her to the door casing, and ran his hands all over her body, as he said, "I want you,

Charity. You're so beautiful. I need you. Come on, baby, you know you want it, too. You always have. You're just like the others, but you've been afraid to show it. I can teach you; I can show you things."

Charity pushed and struggled, but he had her arms pinned down to her side, again. Muscles he had strengthened over the years as an athlete were too much for her. When he pulled back from the hard kiss that was bruising her mouth, she cried out. "Tucker, stop!" But he forced her inside the door, crushing his mouth once again on hers. He was about to kick the door closed behind him, when suddenly he was grabbed by the back of his jacket and tossed outside like a rag doll. He felt his face being pummeled as the blows landed over and over again.

Gabe heard Charity scream his name and remembered there was someone far more important to take care of. He landed one last blow and left Tucker Morrison in a heap on the damp parking lot.

He turned his attention immediately to the girl he had loved all of his life. He prayed she was all right. Gabe was at her side in just a few long strides. He carefully pushed her back into the house, locked the door, and then pulled her into his arms. She came willingly. She was shaking uncontrollably and sobbing hysterically. He held her closely for a few moments then gently pushed her away, just to be able to look at her face to make sure she was okay. He smoothed her long dark hair and looked into her beautiful brown eyes for confirmation that he had stopped the assault in time.

"I'm fine. Really, Gabe. I'm okay," she assured him.

He pulled her back in, this time to comfort himself more than her. His heart was beating hard and the rage had just begun to subside, allowing his breathing to go back to normal. He exhaled deeply, relieved that he had been there to stop it in time. He didn't know what he would have done to Tucker if things had gone any further.

"Tee, my sweet Tee. I'm so sorry."

That brought a little chuckle from her. He had always been able to make her laugh whenever he called her his sweet Tee, which sounded like sweet tea, one of her favorite beverages. She looked up at Gabe through her tears, and smiled weakly, but it was enough to warm his heart. "Can I come in?" he asked softly, not wanting to pressure her into anything.

"Yes, of course. I think I need the company right now. I can't believe that Tucker would act like that. He's always been able to get any girl he's wanted. Why would he try to force me?" Gabe could tell that her whole body was shaking as they moved to sit on the couch.

"Let me get you a glass of wine. You need to relax a little." He knew from past visits that there was always a bottle of Diamante wine on the counter in a welcome basket. And although Gabe had not been in the townhouse in years, nothing had changed. Charity had only invited her girlfriends to her parents' place, but he was here a few times as a kid when his father had been given a bonus for all of his hard work, and the keys had been handed to Mateo to use for the weekend. His hardworking parents were thrilled with the chance to have a mini vacation in this luxury.

He handed her a glass of award winning pinot noir; she eagerly took a sip, and then another, and finally he could see her begin to relax a bit. "I don't know how I can ever thank you, Gabe. And by the way, how did it happen that you were here, anyway -- just at the right time?"

Embarrassed by his sleuthing behavior, Gabe looked down, almost afraid to tell her why he had been there, following her car in the dense fog. But he knew he had to tell her the truth. She could read him like a book. "I just happened to be at The Painted Duck when you two arrived. I couldn't see you, but I recognized your voices." He glanced at her face to see if he could detect the anger that she had been displaying toward him lately. When he did not, he felt safe in continuing. "I actually followed you out the back door, because I wanted to make sure you got home all right in the fog, but then I saw Tucker's car turn into the condo parking lot right after yours. I had a gut feeling that something wasn't right, so I turned in also. I fully intended to stay out of the picture as soon as I knew you were safely inside, but when I heard you scream, my feet carried me forward without my permission." He chuckled to try to lighten the event.

"Did your fists move without your permission, too?" She smiled while her heart was beginning to flutter with a new purpose other than the fear she had recently felt.

"Yeah," he said sheepishly, "I guess, they did."

"I'm sure Tucker will be feeling that lack of permission in the morning. You did quite a job on him."

Gabe rubbed the knuckles on his right hand, then reached to tuck a loose strand of hair behind her ear. The gesture showed a familiarity they had both experienced before. She leaned over, fully intending to kiss him on the cheek in gratitude, but he turned his face in time in order to receive the sweetness he knew he would find on her lips. She pulled back for a moment and then leaned in to complete what they had started. She might not have been able to stop herself, if it hadn't been for the tenderness of her bruised lips, reminding her of what had taken place tonight. Attempted rape was not a laughing matter. What kind of person would she be if she went from Tucker to Gabe within the hour?

"I'm sorry, Tee. I – I just wanted to comfort you. It was very insensitive of me."

"It's okay. But I'm just not ready for that tonight, Gabe. And I'm really tired; I need to sleep. Will you stay – in one of the bedrooms, I mean? I don't want to be alone, and I'm sure the fog hasn't lifted yet."

"Of course, I wouldn't have it any other way." It would take a lot of restraint on his part, because being around Charity had always brought on such intense feelings, but he would be an honorable man because it was best for her.

Charity knew she would need a lot of restraint, because being around Gabe had always brought on such intense feelings she sometimes had found impossible to control, but it was for the best.

Chapter Thirteen

The morning sun was streaming in the unfiltered window, waking Gabe up much earlier than he had intended. He had a little trouble remembering where he was, but when the incident of the previous night came to memory, he bounced out of bed and peeked in on Charity. She was sleeping soundly. He was so relieved he almost cried.

The thought of what could have happened raised his anger all over again. He didn't want to be a reminder any more than necessary to last night's event, so he decided the best course was to slip out quietly and let her sleep. He put on all of his clothes but his shoes, carrying them to the car in one hand, while digging in his pocket for his car key. The sound of the gulls calling as they flew overhead, settling and resettling on the lake, was so raucous he wondered how anyone could sleep. If one of the residents had been looking out the window at that time of the morning, he would have looked like a clandestine lover sneaking away before being discovered by a husband returning from a late-night shift. He prayed no one saw him. They could begin some gossip that might make it back to Spencer and Hope. He had always had the utmost respect for them both, and would never want to hurt them. But then again, he thought, maybe he already had. Hadn't he been the first to be with their daughter when she was only 17 – when they were both 17? And hadn't he taken advantage of her every time she came to him for comfort? And each time they promised not to do it again, hadn't they always found a way back to each other? But the last two years, while she was gone, and after that last time when she had slapped his face, he had tried to do the proper thing, so he had stayed out of her life. It almost killed him every time he heard that she had been home for a visit and he had not so much as glimpsed at her sweet, sweet face.

Now things were different. He could no longer tell himself he was just sexually attracted to Charity. He knew he was way beyond puppy love; he knew he was deeply and almost painfully in love with her -- painfully, because if he couldn't have her for himself, he literally thought he would die. And if he couldn't have her, it would change the course of his life. He would have to move away, leave the grape and wine business that he had grown to love, leave his parents, and everything and everyone around him. Because once he left, he knew he would never come back.

After calling his mother to explain about the weather and why he had stayed in town – he left out the attempted rape and the fact he had stayed at the townhouse – he felt much better. Once he got home, he would talk things out with his mom. She was always so understanding. Of course, there was a lot he planned to leave out, but she would be able to see clearly some things he had not. He also needed reassurance that he was the right man for Charity, and that the two families would approve. Gabe had no idea that their parents had been hoping their two favorite young people would find each other. If he had, some of his choices may have been different. But now, as far as he could tell, his only interferences had been Brick and Tucker, and it appeared, they were both out of the picture. Gabe hoped they never saw Tucker Morrison again, but it was a small town. So he had his doubts. And he still had to convince Charity that it was all right to let a man into her life – that she could still be strong and independent, have her career, and be with a man who would offer her his undying love.

Charity heard the door click, and forgetting that Gabe had stayed over, she jumped up quickly thinking that Tucker was coming back. When she noticed the bed in the room next to hers had been casually made, she recalled all that had happened.

She was so disappointed when she saw that Gabe had left already. She had felt so safe and secure with him there. Gabe was always that to her. Safety, security, comfort. Her knees began to get weak as she heard her own words tumbling around in her head and she realized what she had been thinking. No, it couldn't be! She had always loved Brick!

She grabbed a piece of paper and began to frantically write down all of the words that came to mind when she thought about Gabe. Her fingers were shaking, but once she managed to get the first few words down, it got easier. Then she couldn't write fast enough. Besides safety, security, comfort, she added laughter, joy, strong, handsome, shared interests, family, handsome again, and then passion. Oh, the passion. Sometimes an aching intensity that drove her to him, making her look for excuses to go to him. And even though later she had felt shame because it seemed wrong, especially when they were so young at the beginning, she had felt wonderful at the same time. The last time -- before they had had their fight and she had hurt him so badly with her words and her slap – that time the sensation was so wonderful that she had felt like flying.

She had thought of Gabe as her release, a way to forget Brick, but she had never gone to any other man for that release. In fact, she had managed to get all the way through college without sleeping with anyone. Gabe was her one and only. The clarity of it all was unbelievable. She had been fooling herself all along. A big smile began to form as she realized that she was in love with Gabriel Rivera. And maybe she had been her whole life. Yes, she knew it now. He *was* her Gabe, her rock as she always said in her head. Now how could she convince him that she had changed her mind?

The days passed by in endless work as Charity supervised the construction at the barn. Things were moving along quite nicely, and she was very pleased. She had asked her father to stay away so when he viewed the completion, it would be a nice surprise. So far, he had only known what was going on by looking at papers and blue prints. Since there had been no complications, he had not had to step in or take over, and he had actually complimented her on her thoroughness for detail. The completion of the work was so close now that she had begun to advertise locally. She had compiled quite a list of prospective customers who were eager to see the venue when it was ready.

There was no time to think about Gabe and what he thought of her and what she thought of him – until the hours when she was wrapped up in her covers in bed and no one else was around. Then visions of their stolen kisses over the years, returned full force. Memories of their love making in the barn made her blush, even though there was no one there to see her reddened face. Each day she wondered what she would do or say the next time she ran into him, but he was keeping his distance, and she was not bold enough to ask about him or to call his cell. For now it was enough to know that she had resolved her feelings for him, and once she got through with this big project, it would be time for them to have a long talk. She needed to know where he stood and what he was thinking about her.

Even though the barn construction was moving along smoothly, everything else on the farm seemed to have been jinxed. Vehicles developed mechanical problems one after the other – faulty wiring, flat tires, timing belts, failing brakes, etc. Each day one of the hands reported a piece of equipment that needed to go into the shop for repairs, keeping Gabe very busy. That was bad enough, because it was an irritant and a delay in the day's work. But when things began to go wrong in the winery, it became a real concern for her father. It wasn't close to harvest time yet, so luckily there had been no problems with the grapes, but Spencer began to wonder if he had bad luck or incompetent employees.

One day fifty bags of sugar had sprung leaks, or perhaps were sliced, no one knew for sure, and were spilling all over the floor. Another day he arrived at work to find that large containers of yeast had been spoiled by being left in a warm area of the building after delivery, instead of being transported to the cooler. On a particularly hot day, the air conditioning had failed, putting the soaking grapes with their skins on, creating what was called must, at risk of spoilage. They needed a constant cool temperature for maximum flavor. White wines fermented best between 55 and 70 degrees, and reds between 50 and 80 degrees. Diamante liked to keep their fermenting area at 62 to 65 depending on the grapes they were using at the time. If the temperatures rose too high the flavors could develop an off or bitter taste, and too cold caused the yeast to stop working. It was a big blow to their whole wine making process, and especially this batch, because Spencer had high hopes for the wine competition this year.

Charity could see the strain her father was under, and so she took any small problems of the barn project on herself. As well as supervising the barn, she had begun to look at properties for a wine tasting store outside of the farm. Most vineyards were setting up locations in other cities for those who couldn't travel to their town. Tourist towns like Saugatuck, South Haven, Grand Haven, Muskegon, and Traverse City were a few she had visited. She even checked out a property in downtown Grand Rapids near the convention center and hotels. For now, she was just getting estimates and ideas put together. It was obviously not the right time to approach her father about this plan.

Recently, the next thing to happen in their bad luck stretch, was when an unseasonably early frost settled in for what could become a devastating loss, but the hands went to work and set up the sprinkling system which would run all night long, to keep the freezing moisture from settling on the precious leaves and burgeoning fruit. Spencer got up several times during the night to check on things until he finally felt safe enough to go to bed hoping for the best. As soon as dawn arrived and it was light enough to see, the field hands were in the rows checking on the plight of their grapes. Most of the many acres were fine, but in one area the sprinklers had failed, causing devastating damage to what was to be one of the best variety of grapes they had ever produced. Spencer felt this particular grape could have put them on the world map, but now all was lost. It was not only an expensive blow, but also a huge disappointment. He began to wonder if he was still cut out for the grape growing business.

Charity could feel and see her parents' anxiety. She had tried her best to be cheerful and positive, but not much was helping. Today she was busying herself with some details on the barn restrooms. The tile for the walls and floor had to be selected, and she also needed to make her final choice on the granite for the bar top. It was turning out to be quite a chore to find something that was classy but also keep that rustic feel. She didn't want her customers to feel they were holding a party in a cow barn. She was just about to go to the barn for one last look before calling the tile man, when the phone rang. She turned back to grab the phone on the desk, and was surprised to hear Tucker's voice on the other end.

"Hi, Charity. Do you have a minute to talk?"

"I'm not sure I want to talk to you, Tucker," she said curtly.

"Just give me one minute, please. I've wanted to talk to you in person for a week now, but I didn't want to cause a problem at work. I need to explain. Please listen to me."

She tapped her fingernail impatiently. "Okay, go ahead, I'm listening." 'Why?' she thought to herself. 'I never wanted to see or hear from him ever again.'

"First of all, I am so sorry for what happened."

"You mean what you did – not what happened."

"Yes, what I did. I have been hating myself ever since that night. I can only say, that I have always been attracted to you, and couldn't figure out why you didn't return those feelings. Most females I meet want to be with me. And when you kept pushing me away, it threw me. Maybe it hurt my feelings."

"Your ego, you mean," she said a little nastier than she had intended.

"There's no excuse for what I did, I know. No man should ever treat a woman that way. I'm mortified and embarrassed at my behavior. I'd like to try again, if you can forgive me."

"No, Tucker, that's one thing I can't forgive. Rape is inexcusable and even though I may forgive eventually, I will never forget. So because of that, I never want to see you again. Don't call, don't stop by, don't text or communicate in any way. Do you get that?"

There was silence on the other end. "I want to hear you say it, Tucker. Say you are going to leave me alone."

"Yes, I'll leave you alone. You won't be seeing me ever again," he said with anger. And then he disconnected. Charity was glad he had, because her finger had been poised to do the same.

Chapter Fourteen

The sun was high in the sky, and with no wind and no shade trees, the area around the vineyard was promising to be a scorcher. Even so, Charity decided to walk to the barn. After the phone encounter with Tucker, she needed to clear her mind and try her best to forgive as God would want her to do. She could not imagine why Tucker had behaved as he did; maybe she had never known him at all. She wondered what tales some of the girls he had dated would have to tell if pressed. But just like they had, if it had happened to them, that is, she decided to leave it alone. She didn't want to dwell on what might have happened if Gabe had not been there.

Gabe. She hadn't seen him since that night. When she awoke and found him gone, she was very disappointed. Thinking he had left quietly before she got up just to avoid her, she had decided it was for the best. But there had been that sweet tender kiss, and it had felt so good to be in his arms. Maybe he had felt upset that she had pushed him away once again, but she hadn't been ready for more that night. Couldn't he understand that? Why did men have to have such huge egos, and why was there always only one thing on their mind?

As Charity stepped into a row between the grape vines, she kicked up some dry dust. A grasshopper jumped on her leg and startled her. Lately, she felt like a grasshopper herself, jumpy and skittish. She hadn't always been that way. She used to be self-assured and happy. People enjoyed being around her, because of her easy going nature. But a few years ago things began to change, and as events piled up, one on top of the other, a new personality had emerged. Guarded, careful, distrustful, even afraid at times.

She looked up at the clear blue sky and remembered a date she'd had in college. The dress she had worn that night was the exact color the sky was today. Her roommate said she was a knockout; she said the color was a perfect contrast to her long, dark hair. She remembered the silver hoops she wore in her ears and a turquoise necklace her mother had given her for one of her birthdays, because she said it reminded her of the southwest. The guy Charity was going out with had been wooing her for quite a while and when she felt he was safe, she finally said yes. Apparently, he had thought that because she had agreed to go out with him finally, she had agreed to everything. After their meal, he drove her to a favorite spot to view Lake Michigan. As soon as they parked, she let him kiss her, but in an instant he was all hands. Charity pushed him gently away at first, but then a more forceful struggle began. Before she knew it, her dress was torn and his hands were pulling at her bra. She tried to scream but his mouth was pressed to her lips. She didn't know how she did it with the steering wheel in the way, but she finally managed to get her leg up and knee him. He instantly pulled back, face contorted in pain, gasping for air. He called her several names, said she owed him twenty dollars for her share of the meal, and then threw the car in reverse and drove like a maniac back to her place. She had considered herself very lucky that at least he was man enough to see her home. She shuddered to think what she would have done if he had kicked her out right there in the dark. So when Tucker had tried the same thing, she had freaked out. After the college incident, then seeing Brick and Belle together, she had sworn off from the male species, except for that one time she went home and found herself in the barn with Gabe again. And now here she was, being pulled like a magnet to her childhood friend and lover. Maybe it was all her own fault for letting Gabe have what no other man ever has.

At that point, Charity's musing was interrupted when an indigo bunting swooped down right in front of her path and settled on a grape vine. She stopped instantly to watch the blindingly, iridescent-blue bird peck at an insect or two before he took flight again, almost blending in with the sky except for the rapid movement of his wings. He certainly was glorious. Charity decided to take this sighting as a sign from God that all was well; a sign that He was watching and protecting her as He always had. At that moment she heard voices. Gabe stepped out between the rows quite a distance away from her.

She stood still and watched as he talked with a few of the workers, explaining the proper way to prune the vines. She could hear him saying that this particular area had been hit hard in the freeze and now the dead wood had to be cut back in order to save the vines for next year's production. The dried up wood pulled too much energy away from the good stems. Healthy green leaves needed to collect the sun's rays in order to promote new growth. Charity watched as he confidently went about his job as supervisor. He spoke Spanish as he gave out the instructions; she could tell the men liked and respected him. He had an easy-going, gentle way about him that she had always loved. It was something she needed in her life to balance out the yin and yang. They were perfect for each other – she could see that now. She found herself smiling for the first time today. First, God had given her a beautiful bird as a sign, and then he plopped Gabe Rivera directly in her path. What more could she ask for? She made a motion and stepped forward.

Gabe looked up in surprise and his face immediately broke out in a big grin. He was so happy to see her he thought he would burst. He waved as she moved closer to him. He was thrilled to see her radiant smile reflected back at him.

"Hola! Where did you come from? What brings you here?"

"I wanted to talk to you and a little birdie pointed you out." She laughed at her own private joke. She looked up at the sky and said, "Thank you, God."

When they met in the dusty hot path, Gabe took her hands in his, and looked her deeply in the eyes. "Are you okay, Tee? Really, I mean?"

"Of course, I am, thanks to you. I wasn't ready to talk right away or I would have called, but I really appreciate what you did. Are you through here?"

"Sure, they're ready to go it alone."

"Can you walk with me? I'm heading to the barn, and I really want to talk some things out."

"Of course, I've wanted to see how the barn was coming along anyway." He took her hand, and they began to move at a leisurely pace. His heart swelled now that he knew she was receptive to him once again.

"I need to explain a few things to you, Gabe. And some of it will be hard for me to say, and some of it will be hard for you to hear."

"Okay, go ahead," he said, somewhat apprehensively.

"You know I've had a bad attitude towards men."

"And after Tucker, I can see why, but we're not all like that, Tee."

"I know that now. But I still want to tell you how I got there so you completely understand me. Can

I talk uninterrupted? Because once I get started I need to go all the way to the end."

"Please, I want to hear it all." He was really concerned now. Was she going to ask him to go back to just being friends? Is that what she wanted to say? He was no longer interested in the 'friends with benefits' thing. He wanted her completely. He wanted a life with her. That's all he had ever wanted. He prepared himself for the crushing blow he was sure she was about to deliver.

Charity began at the beginning once again telling about her infatuation with Brick, and then went on to tell about her attempted rape in college. And then she moved on to Tucker and how he had manipulated her, and this time the description of his force and almost rape brought tears. "I'm not sure exactly what he wanted, but he said several times that he had to accomplish something for his father in order to get backing to buy The Duck. I'm beginning to think he was using me, as a way to gain access to information about our winery. You know his father has tried several times to buy Dad out. There's bad blood between them. He's tried some horrible things to get my father to sell. Land for grapes is at a premium now, and it's hard to come by. He went so far as to go to the Township with false claims of business violations and property line infringement. I know my parents were less than thrilled when I went on my first date with Tucker. But they decided not to let the sins of the father visit the son. Now, I wish they had forbid me to see him."

Gabe laughed, "You know you would never have listened, and it would have sent you straight to his arms. You've always had a rebellious streak. Oops, sorry, I'm not supposed to speak. Proceed."

"Anyway," she said slowly as she smiled at him, "I began to be a man-hater, or so I thought. But I just could not stay away from you, and that made me crazy and angry at myself. It was as if I had no will of my own. I thought I had lost my self-control. But after the incident with Tucker, when I woke up in the morning and you were gone, I missed you. I missed you a lot, so I made a list."

"A list, about me?"

"Shh," she hushed, placing her finger on his lips, "no speaking. Yes, I made a list about you." She found this part a little more difficult to say. They continued a few steps in silence, and then she retrieved her voice again. "It was a list of all of the words that came to mind whenever I thought of you. It was supposed to be a pro and con list, but I noticed there was not one negative word on the paper. I've only thought of you in a good way my whole life, unless I was projecting my own bad feelings onto you. Does that make sense?"

"I – think so."

"Whenever I felt bad about myself, I blamed you for making love to me, and as a result, making me love you. I felt guilty because I had convinced myself I loved Brick."

They had arrived at the barn door, and miraculously there were no workers around. "Wait, did you say you love me?" asked Gabe.

He held his breath, waiting for the answer as Charity slowly took out her key to the barn, slid the door open, and walking backwards, pulled Gabe in by the front of his shirt. She never even noticed the newly finished interior, because all she could see were his eyes, as she drew him nearer. She felt as if she were slipping deep into his soul. She knew everything about him, and he knew everything about her. It was obvious, they were one soul. He reached behind him and slid the door closed, then he locked them in so the world would not intrude.

Finally she answered, "Yes, Gabriel, I love you. I always have. There's never been anyone else. I've never *been* with anyone else." He was shocked but very pleased to hear that she was his alone. Charity kissed him with a slow lingering kiss. It felt so good; he wrapped his arms around her and pulled her in so tight that it seemed as if they had merged into one.

"Oh, Tee, I've been waiting since we were twelve to hear you say that. Is it true? You love me?" He placed his hands on each side of her face, gazing at his beautiful Tee with wonder. "You know, I'm crazy about you. I love you," he whispered.

Charity took Gabe's hand and led him up the newly enclosed staircase to the love nest that was waiting for them. The one Gabe had prepared just in case he could convince her to go up the steps with him one more time. He had wanted to show her that his intentions were for love and not just to ease her pain or to help her through a crisis.

Their lovemaking was full of passion as they each tried to express their long pent up feelings. When they were through and they were lying languorously in each other's arms, they talked softly about the past events. They wondered what their parents would say about them openly becoming a couple for the first time. Gabe confessed to seeing his mother and father exchange a glance at the dinner table when they were all together. He thought her parents were in on the matchmaking, too.

"I think they've been rooting for us all along."

Gabe looked at his beautiful Charity once again. He couldn't believe how lucky he was and how wonderful everything had turned out. Even after Tucker Morrison had almost spoiled it all. They dozed for a few moments and let the luxurious afterglow overtake them.

When Gabe woke, he took the opportunity to watch her sleep. Over the years, he had seen her change from child to wild teen to loving woman, and he had changed right along with her. He loved the woman she had become and at that moment he thought he couldn't possibly love her any more. He needed her again, he had to kiss her or he would die. But as he leaned forward to caress her gorgeous face and neck, he stopped, alert to his surroundings; he thought he smelled something. He sat up, and for a moment, he was still as he let his senses sort it out.

She detected his movement and did the same. Their eyes got wide as they both yelled one word – "Fire!"

Chapter Fifteen

They each scrambled to find the tossed clothing that they had removed in haste, Gabe pulled on his jeans and ran downstairs barefoot, with Charity close behind in nothing more than her underwear and his shirt. With her tousled hair wildly flying behind her, she made it down the steps in record time. They stood in the center of the newly refurbished barn and looked frantically around. There didn't seem to be any sign of flames or smoke, and the newly installed sprinkling system had not even been set off.

"What is it? Where?" Gabe ran from corner to corner, looking for any sign of fire.

"It seems to be getting stronger. Outside!"

They ran to the door, struggling to unlock it. They both pulled, sliding the large bulky door to the side, and were shocked to see a pile of construction rubbish in roaring flames. Gabe pulled the fire extinguisher off the wall which was hanging to the right of the door, and ran towards the fire. "Grab the hose and get some water over here. Then call 911."

Charity ran in the dry dusty earth, not even feeling the pickers from the Canadian thistle growing next to the barn; she quickly unwound the hose from the reel. 'Why of all times had they chosen to put it back neatly?' she wondered. She cranked the faucet wide open and ran back toward the fire, spraying water as she went. Gabe had put most of it out, but she continued to wet everything down to make sure all of the hot spots were gone. When they were sure they had it under control, they called the police department.

"There's no way this started on its own. I'm fairly sure a worker would not have tossed a cigarette in the pile. That's suicide. They would not want to get caught in the barn any more than we would. And we've always strictly prohibited smoking on the job. In fact, your dad won't even hire a smoker. The risk is too great, especially in the fall when the vines and weeds are so dry."

"You think someone did this on purpose?" Charity was skeptical, but she realized anything was possible.

They heard car tires and saw flashers as a sheriff deputy pulled onto the lane that led back to their site. They were relieved to see that it was Deputy Tim, as he was known around town. He was Charity's father's age and knew them both very well. He just happened to be driving down the road on his rounds when he saw the smoke and decided he'd better check it out. As far as he knew, no one had requested a burn permit. A second later a call came in from dispatch. He listened to their story, and then assessed the situation, making sure there was no need to call the fire department. When one field caught on fire, it could spread across several miles and ruin an entire crop of grapes for years to come. Fire was always a serious business around here. Tim said he would have to call someone in to assess the pile of rubbish, but he was pretty sure it had been purposely set. Arson was a felony, he said. They would need to get to the bottom of things.

Tim cleared his throat in a polite gesture. "Someone will be out soon. You might want to get more presentable." He chuckled, remembering his younger days. He knew these folks had been doing more than checking out the new construction.

"Ooh – uh – let me just run inside for a moment." Charity clutched Gabe's shirt tightly to her chest with one hand while holding down the shirttails with the other, hoping the length covered what was intended to be seen by no one other than herself, and now Gabe. She turned a brilliant shade of red, as she ran in the barn.

Tim turned to Gabe, and said, "I always knew you two were made for each other." He gave Gabe a light pat on the back, winked, and walked back to the now flameless pile.

Gabe followed Charity inside. When he came up the steps, he saw her searching for all of the different parts of her clothing that had been scattered around the room during their frantic disrobing. Gabe had to look for a few things himself, but he didn't mind at all waiting for Charity to remove his shirt and return it to him. In fact, he rather enjoyed the show. Suddenly they both burst out in laughter.

"Gabe, just imagine, all the times we were here doing the same thing we just did, and we always got away with it. But when we finally declare our love for each other, we're caught. Now the whole town will know."

"I guess we'd better call your father to come out, and hope we can explain ourselves before he hears from someone else." He grinned, and pulled her in to him for one more kiss before the throng of investigators, police, and firemen arrived, most likely accompanied by a reporter. There was never anything to write about around here, so even a hint of an unexplained brush fire would get a paragraph in the local paper.

Spencer showed up a few minutes later. After he was sure no one was hurt, he waited patiently to hear the report of the incident. Charity's father was surprisingly understanding about the fact that they had been in the barn together when the fire was discovered. They left out important details, and let him think they were checking out the almost finished project. A few things were mentioned by the fire chief as far as safety. Why didn't the sprinklers go off? The smoke alone should have activated it. And why were all of the batteries for the new smoke alarms removed? It looked like someone had planned to burn down the whole barn, but when he arrived and found Gabe and Charity inside, he had decided to set the brush pile on fire instead. Apparently, he had not intended to become a murderer as well as arsonist.

"Any enemies you can think of?" asked Chief Thompson.

Charity jumped. She had been thinking of her last conversation with Tucker. He had been so angry.

Was he capable of such an act? Did he set the fire knowing they were inside? Would he do that just because she didn't return his feelings?

"I had a pretty heated conversation with Tucker Morrison earlier today. But I can't imagine him going to this extreme to get back at me," she said.

"Tucker? Can't imagine it," said the Chief. "But I'll look into it. You might want to make your report with Deputy Tim. He'll handle the investigation." He walked away to make some notes on his tablet.

Gabe took her hand. "I think they're through with us. Let's walk a little to think this out."

They walked quite a ways in silence, automatically heading to Owl Creek where they had spent so much time as kids. It was where Gabe had first kissed her when they were twelve. They sat on a large flat rock that had been there as long as Charity could remember.

"What do you make of what just happened?" asked Charity.

"I'm not sure whether it's Tucker or not, but look back on all of the problems we've had. Sugar in my gas tank, failed air conditioning at the winery -- "

" -- failed sprinklers during the freeze," added Charity. "And what about the mechanical failures, spilled sugar, and my flat tires? Someone is after us, aren't they? Diamante Wines, I mean. It might not have anything to do with us. Maybe someone's after Dad." She ached at the thought of someone trying to hurt her wonderful father.

"Gabe, ever since I've come home from college, it's been one trauma after another. But you were always there to steady me, except when I was fighting your strength. I apologize for each and every time I have ever pushed you away. If I could do it all over again things would be much different."

They smiled at each other with their newly acknowledged love. "We've known each other since we were kids, and I've always loved you. You know that, right?" asked Gabe softly.

Charity looked at this amazing man she had almost let get away, and nodded. "I do now. I think I've always known, actually, but I just didn't want to accept it."

He took her hand and began to rub his thumb along her palm, creating a most delicious sensation. "When we go back, we're going to have to tell the whole story. It might be awkward – no, I know it's going to be awkward, but we can leave out some of the more private things." He smiled at her sweetly, praying their secrets wouldn't come out. "I'm hoping our parents will understand that I've always had good intentions, so I want to go back with some good news, to lessen what has just occurred."

Suddenly Gabe slipped off of their favorite rock, and with one knee on the ground, he looked at Charity with his eyes misting over. He reached in his pocket and pulled out the gum wrapper ring that they had made together when they were kids, pretending to be husband and wife. Charity began to cry when she saw it. He was thrilled that she remembered. He was so full of love, he thought he would burst.

"Gabe, what are you doing?" She couldn't believe he had kept that ring all of these years.

He held it out to her, saying, "I know you're against marriage, and you think all men are jerks, idiots, fools, and whatever other name you have used, but I promise I'll try my hardest not to be one of them. I'll probably hurt you somewhere along the way, I'm a man after all, and we never totally understand women, but I am so in love with you. But if I fail, I promise to always do my best to make it up to you. Will you consider breaking your vow to remain single, and become my wife?"

There was silence for a moment. To Gabe it was more than a moment- it was an eternity. He felt he had to fill the gap with more words. "If you don't want marriage, I'll live with you in sin, and believe me, my folks would be very unhappy about that relationship. Trey would probably send me to the hospital, but I'm willing to take you any way you want me. I've been saving for a house of my own, and I almost have the down payment. If your father doesn't kill me first, I believe he'll let me keep my job here. We'd make a great team at the vineyard. What -- "

"Gabe, stop talking," laughed Charity. "I've never heard so many words coming from your mouth, before. You've won me over. I'm ready to retire from spinsterhood. Yes, yes, a thousand times yes. I'll marry you."

Gabe ceremoniously placed the paper ring on her finger, before he raised her up to her feet, and then sealed it with a kiss. She entwined her arms around his neck and promised herself to never let him go. Gabe – her rock.

She held her finger up for inspection, in the way that all women looked at their diamonds, and declared the Wrigley paper and foil ring to be absolutely beautiful.

They walked back to the farmhouse with their arms around each other's waists. Charity was amazed that he had had this ring in his pocket.

"Gabe, I don't understand how you knew that you would propose. Why did you have that ring on you today? We hadn't planned any of this – meeting in the field, the barn," she blushed, "the fire, and now here with you at the creek."

"I've kept it in a keepsake box in my sock drawer, along with a few little army men, and some Boy Scout patches. For some odd reason, this morning I opened the box and when I removed one small soldier, it fell out. I'm not sure why, but I decided to put it in my pocket, maybe as a way of being closer to you. Serendipity?"

"No, I think not. More like God's plan coming to fruition," added Charity. And just as she said that, an indigo bunting flew right in front of them both, singing his little canary-like trill. "And there's your answer." Gabe looked at her questioningly, but he began to grin with joy when she told him about her recent visit from the brilliant little bird as she was walking to the barn.

"I think it's a sign that we are meant for each other," he added. "God selected us when we were very young, and he's happy that we finally figured it out." They paused in their walk for another long kiss, and then another, and another. They had not paid attention to how close to the house they had gotten, but judging by the fluttering curtains at the kitchen window, declarations of their love to Charity's mother would not be necessary.

Chapter Sixteen

The old farmhouse at Diamante Vineyard was filled with family and their friends who were affected by the events. Spencer and Hope, Charity and Gabe, Mateo and Maria, and Trey. Even Belle and Brick had dropped everything and driven in when they heard of the possible arson. Spencer thought the family should be together as they tried to figure what had happened and why. They were all seated around the large family table.

Spencer began the meeting by saying, "I know you've all heard about the fire at the barn. And although it was small and was extinguished quickly -- thanks to Gabe and Charity's quick action -- it could have been much worse. We have to look at it as a serious threat. The question is why."

Gabe stood up and began to pace; he had other things he really wanted to say, but the fire at the barn was taking center stage now. "Charity and I looked back at all of the trouble we've been having lately, and it all began when she first returned from college. First, her tires were flattened which in itself seemed harmless, but a little while later someone put sugar in my gas tank. It didn't get there by itself."

"And the air conditioning failure, when we had just had it serviced," said Trey. "And don't forget about the sprinkler failure on the night of the frost. All innocent occurrences until you add them together." He had been clenching his fists until the knuckles turned white. The thought that someone had it out for their family had sent him into a rage.

Spencer was concerned with his son's demeanor. This *was* important, but he didn't want Trey to get all worked up. "Take it easy, son; we'll take this one step at a time until we can figure it out. At this point we just need to talk it out."

Brick was the calmest of the group, as he used his analytical mind to sort out the facts. "Individually, each thing that happened does not point to sabotage. There's no reason for it." He saw Gabe and Charity shift their bodies and felt the tension as they looked at each other. "Is there? Gabe, is there a reason that you know of?"

Gabe looked at Charity wondering how much she wanted him to say. "Well—I, uh --"

Charity saw his discomfort, and decided it was time to say it herself. "What Gabe is trying to say, is that Tucker Morrison tried to rape me." She felt the tears begin and forced them to stay at bay.

A coffee cup clattered, shocked looks and gasps passed between the women, Spencer slammed his fist on the table, and Trey raised himself up, pushing back his chair with a scrape on the wood floor, now more angry than ever. "I'll kill the son of a --"

Mateo added, "I knew something was wrong, but I couldn't quite figure it out. Tucker was always hanging around, trying to be friendly with the workers. He even passed out some free drink and appetizer coupons for The Duck to the guys. Said he planned on owning it soon and hoped to see them there. And all the time, he just wanted to be on the lot so he could cause trouble. He'll never come near my men again!"

"Wait, wait. Please, everyone, I'm fine. It's over and done with. Gabe was there to save me. He gave Tucker a beating, and we left him bleeding on the pavement."

"Are you okay, mija?" asked Hope.

"Yes, mama. I'm good, really."

"Oh Charity, why didn't you come to me? You can tell me anything. I'm your sister," said Belle with concern.

"Thanks, Belle, but I didn't want to worry you, with the baby on the way. I handled it, with Gabe's help, that is." The look that passed between Gabe and Charity was not lost on the family.

Brick waited a beat for it all to settle in and then said, "Can you tell us what happened, without going into details, of course -- if it doesn't upset you too much, that is."

Charity explained how she had run into Tucker at The Painted Duck, the advances he had made, and how she had thought she would get him off her back with one date. But then she'd agreed to another, and he took the second date to mean more. She went on to say that he had tried to force her at the condo on the night the fog was so thick that she couldn't drive home. But Gabe had been at The Duck also that night and had decided to check on her. He got there just in time to stop the assault.

"The jerk," said Trey. "I never liked that guy. He was too full of himself, even as a kid."

"Tucker contacted Charity the morning of the fire," said Gabe, continuing on with the story. "He wanted to see her again, said he wanted to apologize, and when she shut him down, he got very angry. It was later that afternoon, when we were at the barn, that the fire started. Coincidence? Probably not."

After listening to their comments, Brick decided it was time he take the role of attorney and offer his advice. "Okay, everyone, I've been taking notes. I'm sure you'll each be called in for statements about what you know. Just be sure to be concise and tell them everything. Charity, it's up to you as to how far you want to go with your part in this, but it would make for a good case against Tucker. Then we'll have to wait for the investigation results," said Brick. "If the police don't move on this, we have enough evidence to go after him for attempted rape. He was caught in the act, and Gabe is our witness."

Charity experienced the same fear of pressing charges and going to trial that most women do. Putting her life on public display was not anything that appealed to her at all. "I'm not sure I'll want to do that. I wasn't hurt, and he was stopped in the act. Let's see how the rest plays out."

"Of course, baby," said her dad. He was clenching and unclenching his jaw, a sure sign of his distress. "But I know one thing, he'll pay one way or another." The men at Diamante were not going to be very forgiving when it came to someone hurting one of their women.

Hope jumped up and grabbed a bottle of wine that was always nearby. "I think we each need something to calm our nerves."

"Make it a good one, Mrs. Henley. Charity and I have something else we want to say." He winked at her. His future mother-in-law knew what was coming, and got a big grin.

"I hope it's going to be good news," said Trey, "we could use some about now."

The glasses were filled all the way around, with the exception of Belle and Trey – Belle because of her pregnancy, and Trey because he had sworn off alcohol. After his latest bender he had decided that it was time to quit. The Henley family plus the three Riveras had moved to the family room to be seated around the unlit fireplace where they could feel more connected.

Mateo looked at his lovely wife, Maria, and raised his eyebrow in a questioning look. Spencer glanced at Hope, quite nervous, now. He had a feeling that Gabe was going to move on to better pastures – maybe he had found a choice job somewhere else. He couldn't bear to lose Gabe at this juncture, with all of the trouble they'd been having. He was an excellent crew foreman. He had studied hard over the years and really knew his stuff when it came to growing grapes. He had proven himself time and time again. Mateo and Gabe, as well as Trey, were the only reason they had stayed afloat this season. All three had given one hundred and ten percent to keep Diamante in business. They would not be going to the wine competition this year, and he was very disappointed, but at this point he was more concerned about whether or not Diamante could survive these blows -- the air conditioner and sprinkler failures being the most devastating. If he had known what was to come, he would never have given Charity the go-ahead on the barn renovation. Spencer held his breath as Gabe began to speak.

"First, of all," began Gabe, "I want to say that I've always been so thankful at the way you, Spencer and Hope, have treated me and my family. We came from nothing and you gave us a home, here."

'Here it comes,' thought Spencer, 'he's about to drop the other shoe and leave us.'

"I realized," he went on, "at an early age, that it was all due to my father's hard work and dedication, so I wanted to grow up to be just like him. Soon, growing grapes became my passion. I studied on the side online and by taking courses at community college. It wasn't long before I discovered that what my dad has is an incredible instinct, with people and wine. I might never be as good as he is, but I want to continue to learn so I can be the best grape grower in Michigan.

"Mr. Henley, other than my father, you have taught me everything I know. I watched how you treat your hired help and the respect and love they have for you, and I promise to always behave in that same manner, if you'll keep me on, that is."

'Keep him on? What is he talking about?' thought Spencer.

Having gone through this same thing only a few years earlier, Belle was beginning to catch on. She glanced at Charity, and knew by the excited but nervous look on her face, that it was true. Belle was thrilled, but she did her best not to give away the surprise announcement she knew was coming.

"Charity and I have known each other since we were children, making mud pies, swimming in Owl Creek, and running through sprinklers on a hot day. Sometimes we got along great, and like most children, sometimes we fought a little, but we always came back to one another. Charity has always been very special to me, and from the time I was about 12, I knew that she was the girl for me. It took her a little longer to figure that out, but --"

"Oh, Dios mio, can it be?" asked Maria. She clutched both hands to her chest and waited for the rest.

" – this afternoon I asked her to marry me, and she said yes."

"Gracias, Jesus." Hope and Maria hugged each other with tears flowing.

"Finally," said Hope.

Charity's eyes misted over as she watched Gabe struggle to prove his worth and to show their parents that it was the right thing to do. When she couldn't stand it any longer, she went to Gabe's side. She held up her paper ring, and said, "It's just temporary, -- oh, it is, isn't it, Gabe?"

"Of course, it is, silly," he laughed, and then he kissed her right in front of everyone, no longer caring who or what they thought about their engagement. He looked at each of their faces. He saw shock and surprise, but more than that, he saw happiness.

Belle was the first on her feet, even though moving around had begun to get a little more cumbersome, with the soon-to-arrive baby. "Oh, my sweet, sister, I'm so happy for you."

Hope was next, as she whispered in Charity's ear, "I've been waiting for this for a long time."

Spencer shook Gabe's hand and then gave him a bear hug. "Welcome to the family, son. I thought you were leaving me for a moment. Instead I find out that I am giving you my daughter. But I'm thrilled."

As each member of the family passed on their congratulations, it became apparent that they all knew what Charity hadn't. She and Gabe were meant for each other. It had been in the stars, maybe since their birth. Charity felt at peace for the first time since she had discovered Brick was no longer going to be hers. The day her childhood fantasy went up in smoke had changed the course of her life, or so she had thought. Instead, that day had just put her on the right path – the one God had chosen for her.

Maria was standing with Gabe, talking softly to him, telling him how he should cherish the woman he had been given, telling him how she knew he was a good man and would be the kind of husband she and his father expected of him. Then she kissed him on the cheek and said "I am so happy for you, my son. I know you have loved her for a long time."

Mateo clasped Gabe's hands in his own. They were the hard-working hands of the son he had been raising to be a good provider. He was proud to see it all come together; he was so happy for his son and the woman he had chosen to be his wife. "Congratulations, son. Now, go get her a decent ring!"

The next day Gabe and Charity went to the sheriff's department to offer a formal statement of what had occurred at the barn fire, from their perspective. They had agreed ahead of time to tell everything they knew, including Tucker's aggression to Charity, because that showed motive, but they kept it low key.

"And it was really more the fact that he was rejected, I think," said Charity.

Deputy Tim looked her right in the eye and said, "Are you sure that's all it was? Because if there was anything more we can prosecute separately from the vandalism."

"No, I don't want to do that. He was rough, yes, but it had only gotten to a forceful kiss before Gabe intervened. I just brought it up in order to explain our theory about why Tucker might have done some of these things. I think he was jealous of Gabe. He might have been following me around and knew that we were a couple, well, sort of – we were trying to figure things out, I guess you could say."

"Look," said Gabe, "I've never liked Tucker. But I never pegged him for someone who would vandalize, or worse yet, force a girl. I know he doesn't seem like the logical suspect, but who else could it be? He was on the premises more than once. He often made excuses to stop by and talk to Charity when he could have called. He was seen roaming around in the winery talking to the guys."

"Any possibility it had to do with wine competition?" asked the astute deputy.

"Anything's possible, I'm sure. But the question is why, when he had already told Charity he wasn't interested in growing grapes like his dad. He wants to buy The Painted Duck."

"Really? Well now, you've given me a few things to go on. Thanks so much for coming in. And Charity, I know it was difficult to tell me what you went through with him, but I'm always here if you want to press charges."

"Thanks, Tim. I appreciate it. But for now, I'm going to let it go. I've tried to put it behind me, but if you hear of it happening to anyone else, you can use my statement then."

On the way out of the building, Gabe said, "What do you think? Could it be Tucker?"

The woman he loved raised an eyebrow and looked at him sideways. "Who else?" Charity replied bitterly.

A few days later Deputy Tim stopped by Spencer's office. He asked that Charity be present, also. "I thought you might want to hear the update from me. The Fire Chief ruled the fire an accident, not arson. It was started with a cigarette butt. After questioning some of the construction workers, they all pointed to one man who often smoked on the job when the boss wasn't around. He was a migrant worker, and after the fire he was never seen again. He just didn't show up for work. We're thinking he might have been illegal and didn't want to face any questioning. Jim Holtz has always been careful about who he hires, or I wouldn't have used him for any type of construction work, myself, but this one might have slipped through the cracks. He could be anywhere at this point."

"Does that mean you've closed the case? What about the vandalism?" Spencer's fury was shown in his complexion as it turned a bright shade of red. "I've lost a lot of money this year, Tim."

"I know you have, Spence. No, we didn't stop there. We used the fire to draw out the real culprit. We hauled Tucker in for questioning and threatened an arrest. He didn't know that we knew it wasn't arson – and neither did his father."

"Are you kidding?" gasped Charity in shock. She was beginning to piece together the string of events.

Tim went on. "As soon as we mentioned arson and a possible arrest, Dan Morrison was down to the station in a New York minute. He was not about to let his son go down for something he did."

"Dan? Impossible," sputtered Spencer. "I can't stand the guy, but vandalism? Never!"

"It turns out that it is possible. Of course, he never did anything himself. He said he had asked Tucker to move in on Charity in order to have a reason to hang around and gain some information on your wine making operation. In exchange, he promised to buy The Painted Duck for Tucker. Dan was hoping to best you at the competition. But then he had another brilliant idea. He would try to prevent you from showing up and entering a wine at all, so he hired someone to flatten tires and put sugar in a gas tank, spill sugar in the winery and ruin your yeast. He then proceeded to damage the air conditioner and the sprinklers causing even more destruction. He's one of your new hires this year. I suspect he was a plant to begin with."

"What's going to happen to Dan?" asked Spencer.

"He'll have to face charges in front of a judge, so it all depends on which judge it is. I assume it's going to be one of his poker playing buddies, so chances of him getting anything more than paying restitution or doing community service are slim. His hired hand has also left the state, so that's a dead end. I spoke to family members he left behind in his haste. His wife and children are now dependent on others to take care of them. A real loser, in my book."

"What about Tuck?" Charity could hardly contain herself. She almost hated him now for using her like that.

"Tucker is humiliated that his father went to the extent he did. He really didn't know anything about the vandalism. He was just told to get close to Charity, and ever since he was a kid, he's always done whatever his dad has told him to. Dan is a real piece of work."

"Tell me about it," said Spencer. "I've had to live next to him for thirty years."

"Well, folks, I've got more loose ends to tie up, and endless paperwork, but it seems as though we've solved your mystery. I'll let you know if there are any updates or changes in the story, but I think we can close this one, unless Dan goes to trial which I highly doubt."

"Thanks so much, Tim," said Spencer and Charity together.

"I'm sorry about all of this, Spence. I know you were looking forward to the competition this year." Deputy Tim tipped his hat and went back to his duties.

Epilogue

The barn was as gorgeous as any barn could possibly be. In true Martha Stewart style, just as Charity had requested, white lights were strung everywhere, casting an ethereal glow on the decorations and, most importantly, the bride. Charity was pleased with what she had accomplished, and her father had praised her highly for sticking to the project in light of all that had happened.

They had made their goal of completion in time for the fall harvest. That was when most people start to think about fall color tours followed by wine tasting, so the ads placed in the local papers had already brought about many reservations.

"If this first event goes well, we can at least have a practice run behind us," said Charity, biting her lip. She was extremely nervous for the wedding to begin.

She had checked and double-checked to make sure everything was in place. She would not settle for anything less than perfection.

"Charity, relax," said Sid, "You're stressing too much. Let the caterers, wedding planner, and maid of honor do their jobs. It's out of your hands, now. Now, you'd better get dressed. Jeans won't do for your first wedding." Her best friend gently pushed her forward, forcing her feet to move from their spot where she had been giving her last-minute inspection.

"Okay, okay. I'll go. It's hard to turn it over to someone else now, after all of these months. But you're right. No one wants to see me with my hair in a clip and my work clothes on. Come with me. I'll show you my upstairs loft."

Sid went upstairs with Charity, expecting a rough room with bales of straw and was surprised to see what looked like a bedroom ready for romance. She raised an eyebrow and laughed. "So this is the famous barn loft I knew nothing about. How did you manage to keep it from me all these years?"

"Sorry, Sid. It just seemed too private at the time. I should have discussed it with you, but I was so confused about Brick and Gabe, and I was embarrassed, I guess. Gabe and I never told anyone. Looking back, it might have been easier if I had asked for your opinion."

"I don't know if I would have had the proper input. At age seventeen, you really don't have enough knowledge of the world to be giving an opinion on someone else's love life. I might have made things worse. Anyway, it all worked out. I'm so happy for you two. A perfect match, in my opinion, and I'm old enough now to give one." Sid laughed and then pushed Charity toward her dress. "Come on, it's getting late, and we have to do your hair, yet."

Downstairs, the caterer was arriving with lots of food, the flowers were being delivered and placed in the perfect locations selected by the bride, and the wine sommelier was setting up behind the bar, allowing some wines to breathe and others to chill. He was there to serve but also to encourage the guests to sample new varieties that could turn into sales after the wedding. No wine orders would be filled on the bride's day, but a guest could take home an order sheet and plan for their next visit. Since the sommelier had recently received his certification and had been hired by Diamante Wines for their wine tasting room, it was more or less a practice run for him, also.

Word was out that the groom had arrived and was getting dressed in the men's room. Although the barn would seem like a very casual setting to most, it had been transformed into a fancy upscale reception hall. The bride and groom had decided to go all the way with formal attire – so tux for him and a long-flowing white dress for her. Red roses were placed on all of the tables in low, round, glass bowls. A string of white lights had been run down the length of each table. The guests would be seated at the tables for the wedding ceremony in order to prevent having to move tables and chairs around afterwards for the reception. The musicians took their places near the wedding arch which was placed on a raised stage. When the ceremony was completed, the arch would be moved to the side, so the band could set up for the music and dancing to come. The bride had requested that the musicians play a classical piece for the ceremony and then swing into their traditional Mariachi music for the Mexican-American reception.

"I hope Dan Morrison doesn't give us any problem when he hears the music floating across the fields," worried Charity.

"Are you kidding? He's afraid to make any kind of move that would be confrontational. He's lucky he's not in jail!" Sid was furious when she discovered what her friend's family had gone through. "And that Tucker – I'm never speaking to him again for as long as I live."

"All over and done with, Sid."

"You're right. It's just still pretty new to me. I can't believe you left me in the dark for so long."

"Sorry. Do you forgive me?"

"Of course. Always and forever." Sid looked at Charity in the mirror. "There. How's that?" she said with one last push of a hair pin. "I always envied your Mexican heritage. You've been blessed with such beautiful hair, so thick and long. When it's put on top of your head like this, you look like a queen."

"Thank you, Sid. You're so sweet. Now will you help me with this zipper?"

"Of course. That's what the maid of honor is for," she said to the bride. "Do you have all of the parts? Something old, something new, something borrowed, something blue?"

"The dress is new, my grandmother's diamond earrings are old, I borrowed your bracelet, and blue – oh no, I forgot blue."

They glanced around the room for something they could use, but just then, there was a knock on the door at the bottom of the stairs. Sid ran down and returned with a gift wrapped with a beautiful silver bow. She smiled slyly and said, "From the groom."

Charity had missed seeing Gabe today-- they had decided to be traditional and not see each other until the wedding -- so she eagerly tore into the box.

264

She lifted out a silver necklace. The charm hanging from the chain was a tiny indigo bunting with his head raised in song. Charity's eyes misted over. He had remembered. It hung perfectly on the neckline of her dress.

"How did he know the proper length?"

"A little help from a friend," winked Sid. "Now, it's time to go down. I hear the music playing and Gabe just told me the guests are all seated." Little did Charity know, that when she was renovating the barn, she was creating her own wedding venue and reception hall.

Charity looked at her loft room, once again, making sure everything had been put back in place. People were being told they were leaving for a honeymoon in Hawaii immediately following the reception, but only she and Gabe knew that they were planning to spend their first night in the loft. They would sneak back here when it was dark. It would always be a special place, the reasons known only to them. They planned to keep the loft room as a getaway for those times when they needed to be alone, maybe after children were born and the grandparents were babysitting, or during the afternoon when the kids were in school and they needed to get away from the stress of the daily routine. Charity smiled to herself, thinking about all of those times she would make that happen. She took a deep breath. She no longer had any qualms about giving up her single life. She was one hundred percent ready to open the door at the bottom of the stairs and see her handsome groom who was waiting patiently for her on the other side -- waiting to see his Tee, the love of his life.

Sample the first chapter in the next book of The Lighthouse Trilogy.

Owl Creek

The Lighthouse Trilogy Book 3

Chapter One

He could smell dust, spilled beer, and cigarettes, most likely from the previous tenant-- the cigarettes, that is, since he didn't smoke. The beer and dust were definitely his. He hadn't cleaned house in quite a while and spilling had become a habit.

Trey's bones were stiff and achy. He knew it was time to move, but he wasn't able to function quite yet. He slowly opened his eyes, but the light blinded him; it took some effort to focus. He peeked out, closed his eyes again, and then tried to open them one more time. This time he forced them to stay open. When the blurred lines finally became sharper, all he could see was an ant crawling slowly on the carpet carrying a large crumb on his back, most likely from Trey's leftover pizza crust. It looked like an impossible feat for an insect its size, but the ant trudged on with the determination that all ants seemed to have. Trey watched it weave back and forth through the twisted pile of the yarn, with a single purpose in mind -- getting to the other end. Maybe he had a family to feed with children crying and a nagging wife, or maybe it was just the pure willpower needed to find his way out of the carpet maze in which he had unexpectedly found himself trapped.

While watching the ant, Trey wondered why he had never had a family of his own, other than his parents and sisters. But unlike the ant, his willpower had left him the day he returned from Afghanistan. Reflecting back, he realized he had never been much interested in having a wife and kids. He had had too much fun to even consider settling down, and now that he thought of it, willpower had never been his strong suit, either– until he had joined the military. The Marines had browbeat willpower and responsibility into him, but the minute he was discharged, he had thrown everything he had learned out the window. It was back to the good life – parties, booze, and girls -- until recently. Lately, he preferred to party by himself, just him and his vodka. The thought of vodka made him raise himself up off the floor. He pushed up on his elbows and looked for a bottle, but found only one empty one laying on its side on the coffee table.

He suddenly had to pee, so he was forced to get up. The floor was getting rather cold and hard, anyway. Trey weaved unsteadily to the bathroom, relieved himself, drank a large glass of water, and then headed toward the bed of rumpled sheets and blankets in hopes of finishing his sleep in a more comfortable setting. But as soon as his head hit the pillow, his cell phone began to ring. He reached groggily for it, and answered in a gruff, scratchy voice.

"Hello?"

"Where are you?" yelled his sister, Charity. "Dad's having a fit. I can't cover for you again, Trey. Get your butt over here. NOW!"

"Okay, okay. I'm just running behind a little. What's the big deal?"

"The big deal is that you promised Dad you'd be on time from now on. Seriously, Trey, this isn't like you at all. Even through everything, you've always shown up for work. What's going on?"

"Look, can we talk later? I'm trying to get ready, here. Isn't that what you wanted? I'll be there. The grapes can wait." Trey was not normally short with his little sister, but lately she was all over his case. She was trying to prove herself in her new position in the family grape and wine business, but that had nothing to do with him. Trey looked at the clock. It was only eight; couldn't a guy get some shuteye? He closed his eyes for just a few seconds, and the next thing he knew the phone was making that blasted noise again. He reached for it and answered with one syllable. "What?"

"Trey, Gabe here. Are you on your way? It's 8:45. Come on, man. I promised your sister I'd get you here. Grab a cup of coffee from the gas station and come in to work. Make me look good to Charity. I told your dad you're on an errand that I requested you do on the way in. He seemed satisfied with that. But I can't hold out too much longer."

"Okay, okay. Give me fifteen minutes."

"Just get here safely, and then we're going to have a chat." The phone went dead. Gabe had a habit of hanging up without saying goodbye. That was fine with Trey; the less conversation the better. He sat up and placed his long legs on the floor, then dragged himself out of bed, splashed some cold water on his face, and ran his fingers over his short hair. The military cut suited him and so he had kept it. Less fuss. There was no sense in preening in front of a mirror. He was tall and broad-shouldered; his good looks and winning smile always got him whatever he wanted or needed – with his family and with the fairer sex. The girls loved him. He had mastered the art of flirting, and it had served him well. He didn't remember the last time he had been rejected.

He was finally on the road. The gas station coffee was strong, but exactly what he needed. He had even thought to stop at the hardware store on the way by and pick up two pair of pruners, in case his dad asked him what Gabe had asked him to buy and why he was late. Trey was used to lying now. It was becoming easier each time he did it. No problem; they were none the wiser.

His parents, Hope and Spencer Henley, had been so proud of him when he returned from active duty. He had received a purple heart, and a bronze star. It had been hard to take all of their praise, knowing his buddies were still there, and worse, that some had not made it at all. The external wounds had long since healed, just scratches according to him whenever asked, but the wounds that were left inside, would take a longer time to learn to deal with, and would always be a part of him. He knew the memories of what he had seen and done could never be erased, but he intended to try, and right now the bottle seemed to be the only way to achieve that goal.

After Trey had returned from the Marines, he stayed with his parents for a few weeks, because his mother wanted him near. She had to reassure herself daily that he was all right. He still had a slight limp, so she used that as an excuse to baby him. He could tolerate it for just so long, and in an effort to not lose his temper and hurt her feelings, he told them it was time he found his own place. There was some discussion and gentle persuasion, but they really had nothing to say about it. It was his life, he told them. He had led men and made decisions on the other side of the world, he said; he would have no problem making his own bed and buying his own groceries. With Charity still in college at the time and Brick and Belle recently married, he knew his mother was fighting empty nest syndrome. But as all parents must and did, she got used to it, mostly because she saw him every day at the farm, and he made a point of having lunch with her. His mother was the sweetest woman in the world, and he never wanted to hurt her.

Trey found a nice little cottage on Lake Michigan, set back quite a ways from the beach, up high on a dune in a wooded lot, where he could still see and hear the breaking waves. It comforted him like nothing else had since he had returned. The rhythm of the water as it ebbed and flowed from Wisconsin and back was better than going to a therapist or getting a massage. He felt more like himself here than he had in years. The other nice thing was that he could drink to his heart's content, or discontent, as it were. Not every day -- just once in a while at first, when things came crashing in on him. It might be a car backfiring which sounded like gunfire, or the sight of a campfire that triggered memories of burning tanks and jeeps. The sounds of children yelling and shrieking as they played could recall memories of the screams and carnage and was too much to bear. Vodka was the only solution. But in time he began to put an effort into fixing up his place after working at the winery all day. Painting and swinging a hammer gave him great pleasure. And late at night when he couldn't sleep, he would take long walks on the beach. Nature was at its best then, in the dark and quiet. He would pray as he walked, looking up at the bright stars. It made him feel close to that other side of the world, knowing it was the same sky his buddies were seeing when it was night over there. He prayed for their safety and return to their families. He prayed that they were able to leave their demons behind. And then he prayed for himself – that his own demons would shrink and wither away into the night. Usually, by the time he had returned from his walk, he felt better and was able to sleep – a restless sleep, but sleep nonetheless.

In time he had not felt the need to drink, and a sort of happiness had returned. He had even gone to Charity's homecoming, a few family gatherings on July 4th, birthdays, cookouts, and then Charity and Gabe's wedding, and he had not touched a drop. Everyone noticed the difference in him. He realized that they had known he was drinking all along and were just biding their time before they approached him about it. They all breathed a sigh of relief when he had righted himself without their intervention.

But recently something had occurred that had turned his world upside down once again. Trey received a letter from the parents of a best friend he had left behind in Kabul. Dave had ended his tour of duty at the same time as Trey. He had returned home to safety, and then for some reason known only to him, he had re-upped. He was sent to Iraq this time, and after spending the first half of his tour there unharmed, he was struck down by a suicide bomber while on leave in Germany. Learning of his death had put Trey over the edge. He had traveled to Pennsylvania for the funeral, where he had met up with a few old buddies. They all asked, 'What's the sense of it all? The world is going mad and there seems to be no way to stop it.' They drank some beer and reminisced, trying their best to recall only the good times. They had a lot of laughs, but they all knew that the laughter was only covering their pain. And it was just enough to start Trey on his downward spiral again. When he returned home, he had a secret to hide once again. Vodka was now his best friend, because as long as he had enough money for a bottle, it would never leave him.

I would like to thank you, my reader, for following my books in this trilogy, but I have no way of knowing whether you like what I write unless you leave some feedback. If you have a few moments, I would really appreciate it if you would leave a review on Amazon. Only a few sentences are necessary; there's no need to write a book yourself, so don't be scared. Just tell what you like about the book or maybe which character you liked best and why, or perhaps you have other thoughts you'd like to share.

You can type in the title of the book in the Amazon search window or go to my author page and find the book there. The address is:

Amazon.com/author/obrienjane

Look for Owl Creek coming in the fall of 2016.

Thank you so much, Jane O'Brien

CPSIA information can be obtained
at www.ICGtesting.com
Printed in the USA
BVHW041928110419
545282BV00016B/239/P

9 781533 210456